SPIN THE PLATE

Donna Anastasi

Black Rose Writing
www.blackrosewriting.com

© 2010 by Donna Anastasi
All rights reserved. No part of this book may be reproduced, stored in a retrieval system or transmitted in any form or by any means without the prior written permission of the publishers, except by a reviewer who may quote brief passages in a review to be printed in a newspaper, magazine or journal.

First printing

All characters appearing in this work are fictitious. Any resemblance to real persons, living or dead, is purely coincidental.

ISBN: 978-1-935605-39-3
PUBLISHED BY BLACK ROSE WRITING
www.blackrosewriting.com

Printed in the United States of America

Spin the Plate is printed in 12-point Times New Roman

Cover graphic by Mountain Ash Web

Referenced and credited music:

Neil Diamond – *Sweet Caroline* – 1969
Billy Joel – *The Longest Time* – 1984
Enrique Iglesias – *Hero* – 2002

I am grateful for –

The Inspiration for this book, Tom Anastasi who filled in the blanks, and Ellen Bellini, Libby Hanna, and Janet Morrow for sharing their stories.

Ink Angel

Dual Lives

First Date

Meet the Parents

Crusades

The Sentence

Lazy Sundays

Conversion

Confession

The Dream

Epilogue

CHAPTER 1: Ink Angel

Jo boarded the Green Line subway train D at Newton Highlands heading into Boston's Back Bay. With the lunchtime rush, seats were scarce. She spied the last available one and beat a man in a pressed suit to it by one step. He stood, facing her. He grabbed onto the rail above him and gazed over her head out the window. He was clearly tired of standing and even more clearly annoyed at having lost the seat to her.

"What a prick," she thought.

"Longwood" boomed over the sound system. Just five stops to Arlington Station. The train ground to a halt. No one got off. Half a dozen newcomers entered, the doors closed, and the passengers found their spots as the train lurched forward. With no seats vacated, the man remained standing.

"Dyke," he muttered just loud enough for her to hear.

In an instant she was up on her feet, transforming herself from some fat lady into a female version of an NFL linebacker: very big, extremely strong, and surprisingly fast. She was 257 pounds and stood 5' 11" in her Chippewa hikers. She wore a flannel shirt–burnt orange with black checks–and denim overalls. In an inner pocket nestled in the slight dip at her right hip bone and easily accessible from the bib of her overalls, she carried a Beretta 9mm Classic with 10 live rounds. The gun was always with her; she touched it now. She would not allow anyone to hurt her.

"Fuck you," she said loudly and deliberately.

She stared into the man's widening eyes and watched him lower his gaze. He turned away, weaved through the crowd, and headed for the exit. Gripping the side pole, he stood at the doors, waiting, praying for them to open. Part of him felt emasculated, running away from a female, but as he furtively double checked her size, another part of him realized confronting her had been a mistake. The train stopped at Fenway Station, and he bolted through the door. Watching the train pull away, he leaned against the tiled wall and waited for the next D train. It was a valuable life lesson on keeping your mouth shut on the Boston T.

Jo grinned inside and enjoyed the rush of winning, once again. Outwardly, though, she exhibited her "fuck-off" look. She had long ago set her jaw to create an unchanging, distant look with a hint of menace. Surveying fellow passengers, she noticed with some satisfaction the lowered heads and averted eyes intent on newspapers or on some crud ground into the floor.

Jo was satisfied to pull off the illusions of both fat chick and psycho lesbian in one interaction. She invested much energy in keeping men at bay, and these were two favorites in her repertoire. Though she was much more comfortable around women than men, she wasn't gay. Asexual would be a more accurate term. This little incident was simply to hone her anti-social skills.

Her cell phone rang.

"Hey Keisha," she said. Then after a pause. "Yeah, I'm running late. I'll be at I.A. in about a half hour." She pushed the End button.

"Shit," she said hoping to prolong the uneasiness of the commuters surrounding her.

Settling back into her seat, Jo glanced across the aisle and noticed a wiry man in his early 30s sitting across from her. He had brown eyes, tan colored skin, and curly brown hair. The ridges of his brown corduroy pants were partly worn off, and his retro-Nike sneakers were white, scuffed leather with a green swish. Around his neck was a hemp string knotted every three inches with a 3 inch simple wooden cross at the end. She pegged him for a graduate student, because along with the Bohemian look, he also had a copy of the today's Wall Street Journal. He probably attended Boston University or Brandeis.

With an amused look, the man searched her face. He seemed to cut straight through the façade, as if her broad smile was plain and he was sharing in the joke. He looked hard to penetrate her expression and see the features beneath–distinctive cheek bones, long lashes, full lips–imagining what she'd look like if she smiled. His wondering was promptly cut off.

She glared at him. "What the fuck is wrong with you?"

He wasn't afraid. He was fairly certain she was all talk, unless threatened.

"Jesus loves you, you know," he blurted out.

Then thought. "Great opening line, Francis." Still,

he felt obligated to pass on the message.

The train groaned and settled to a halt. "Arlington" came over the loudspeaker. This was her stop.

"Jesus freak," Jo thought as she exited the train.

The walk from the station was the roughest stretch in her day. Normally, she'd stick to the main thoroughfare for the distraction afforded by jostling crowds: clumps of woman in suits and lunch-hour sneakers, shoppers, theatre-goers, and the occasional homeless guy. She'd take either Arlington or Charles Street to Beacon and then follow one of the Nut side streets to get to work. But today she was late and cut through the Public Garden right past the Swan Boats. The park was empty except for a group of pre-school children playing, with a few moms hovering nearby, and an older man seated on a bench nibbling a bologna sandwich.

Jo knew she must avoid downtime: when her mind was allowed to wander it often roamed to dangerous places. She focused on her power, weight, and regimen. She maintained a layer of fat, for protection, around a muscular build. She ate and trained following the practices of a Sumo wrestler. Wearing loose-fitting clothes created the illusion of obesity though she was in top health and extremely strong.

She enjoyed exerting her power to hurt men who deserved it. She found the rush was all the better when it came with an element of surprise. She never tired of seeing that look of bewilderment mixed with pain when she smashed her fist into a man's face. They never saw it coming.

Jo found herself relaxing in the warmth of the approaching afternoon, surrounded by the squeals of laughter from children in an impromptu game of tag and the smell of turning leaves in the air. As her mind started to stray, she wondered desperately, "Why can't I be like everyone else, and be blessed with *repressed* memories?" The images, the pain, every emotion was raw and fresh–time had done nothing to dull the wounds inflicted more than a dozen years ago.

She still could replay each event as though it were a television series rerun. Today episode 62 played in her head: *"The Dollhouse." This one starts out with a little girl sitting on her bed combing light caramel curls with a cherrywood-handled brush and comb and mirror set her Daddy had given her last week. She pulls down a banana curl with the brush and watches it bounce back up in the hand mirror. She examines her face critically, looking hard into her chocolate brown eyes framed by long lashes. She looks up from the mirror as Daddy strolls into her bedroom with a huge and bright pink dollhouse stretched across his open arms, turning to balance it on one arm and a knee, locking the door behind him. A moment later, Mommy raps on the door and says Juliana are you in there? He bellows at the closed door Do you want me to come out! And Mommy scurries away. As he turns back around, a scowl melts into an excited grin. He sits on the floor and shows her all the features; see the closet door and the little dresser drawers that really open.*

She hopes faintly that he's come to play dolls with her. He says to her Daddy has given you a wonderful gift and now...

Jo finally reached work, at 12:45–fifteen minutes before the upscale shop, where she worked as a tattoo artist, opened. It was a two-woman operation called Ink Angels owned by Lakeisha Thomas, with whom Jo had worked for over five years. Lakeisha was a stunning black woman who barely reached five foot two in her three inch heels. As one customer put it, "even her curves have curves." Jo wasn't sure what that meant, but the phrase always came to mind whenever she gazed at Lakeisha's large shapely butt or boobs. Keisha got Jo.

Lakeisha was already inside. Jo tried the door; it was locked, so she opened it with her key. Jo walked in, still fueled with adrenaline over the train incident and agitated over the walk in the park.

"Good morning," Keisha greeted her.

"Fucking prick," she blurted out.

"Go on," Lakeisha said.

"This goddamn clone called me a dyke on the train," Jo complained.

"You know you wanted him to think that," Lakeisha returned.

Jo tried her bad look on Lakeisha. She would have none of it.

"No, no, no. You're not going to give me your fuck off look. Not today, sweetie. Now you go back outside and let's try this again. I don't have time for the 'I hate the world' shit today. Yea, he was a prick for noticing how butch you decided to get, but give me a break. We've got a lot of customers today, and I do not have time for this. So go."

Jo relented, but only because it was Keisha, plus it gave her permission to end the rush. Jo went outside, gulped three deep breaths, and then a fourth, before going back in.

"Good morning," Keisha said glowingly.

Silence.

"Good morning, Jo," Keisha repeated. "And how are you this wonderful day?"

"Fine," Jo returned.

"Okay then. Your first client is coming in right at one," Lakeisha informed her, shifting into business mode. "She wants a tramp stamp."

Jo calculated. "Should take about an hour and a half. Is she a virgin?" Virgin was tattoo shop talk for someone getting a first tattoo.

"Let me check," Lakeisha flipped open the appointment book. "I don't know. Her name is Lauren Greene. A white girl from the suburbs."

Jo went to the treatment area and arranged her ink and needles. The shop had a public waiting area and a more private back room where the tattoos were inked. There was also what Keisha called the employee "break room," which was the size of a walk-in closet and windowless. The public area had walls lined with different designs. The left side was geared toward men, the right for women, and in the center were more gender neutral options. There was a counter with a cash register and credit card machine, as well as several books of more designs, and a book of photos of smiling, wet-eyed Ink Angels' clients showing off their new looks.

Behind the counter were framed copies of their state licenses and a sign that read, "You must be 18. No exceptions. State issued Driver's License, Passport or Military ID needed."

The ringing bells on the door could be heard from the back room. Lauren walked in with her friend Deidra, a regular customer. Lauren had one small seagull tattoo on her ankle and wanted a design on her lower back. Jo could hear Lakeisha sending them back.

"Hey Jo," Deidra said.

Jo gave a neutral look.

Deidra was 32 years old and worked as an office manager at Fidelity Investment Services in the financial district near the 60-story, antennae-topped landmark Hancock Center. Her co-workers considered her to be straight-laced. They had no idea that she frequented bars in Framingham, an urban suburb west of Boston, and hooked up with whatever guy looked tempting. After allowing the man de jour to buy her a few drinks, she would get herself invited to his apartment and generally make a break by dawn. Sometimes she'd hang around until breakfast, and every now and then in a weak moment, she would acquiesce to a second date.

"Deidra," Jo said attempting to sound friendly. "How's the tat?"

"Love it."

Deidra unbuttoned her shirt and pulled over enough of her bra to expose the top of her left breast. A blue and yellow long-tailed lizard was drawn starting from the two o'clock section above her nipple. From a distance it looked to be a cute gecko, but up-close it appeared more serpent-like, venomous.

"I didn't know you got that," Lauren said. "Who's going to see it?"

"Very fortunate men," Deidra laughed.

Lauren also was an employee at Fidelity; she worked in the call center. She was five feet, six inches tall, with natural strawberry blonde hair and green eyes, made even more vivid with tinted contacts. She was taking advantage of the last of the Indian summer wearing a T-shirt, satin shorts, and Adidas running shoes with no-show socks.

"When are you getting some ink yourself?" Deidra asked Jo.

Jo snapped back, responding with a pat answer to the question she heard almost every day. "You know I don't go for that sort of thing."

Visible tattoos revealed too much about a person's past or passion or pain. And, Jo thought, there was no way anyone was going to get lucky enough to see a more privately situated tattoo.

Turning to Lauren, Jo asked. "Do you know what you want for your back?"

"You mean the tramp stamp?" Deidra chuckled, repeating a phrase she'd picked up from Keisha.

"No. Not slutty," Lauren clarified. "But kind of wild. I grew up as the good little Catholic girl. It's been a hard image to shake. My longtime and now ex-boyfriend didn't want me to do this. Now that he's out of the picture, I figure this is the time, before I hook up with someone else who tells me what I can't do."

"Let her design it for you," Deidra said. "That's

what I did."

Lauren looked pained. She'd have this for life. What if she didn't love it?

"Oh, go for it," Deidra coaxed.

Lauren was apprehensive, but she trusted Deidra.

Deidra knew Jo had a keen ability to decipher a vague notion and transform it into a work of art. People sought Jo out for her reputation for creating custom, one-of-a-kind, free-style designs. She used no sketches, no collaboration.

Jo stared hard into Lauren's eyes and already knew more keenly than Lauren herself what she was seeking.

"Ready," Jo said. It was as much an order as a question.

Lauren swallowed hard, all of a sudden feeling nervous.

"I guess."

"Lie face down on the table. Deidra, you can come back in about an hour," Jo commanded.

Deidra knew the drill. "Okay."

She crouched down to face Lauren.

"It will be all right," Deidra said, got up, and left.

Jo commanded. "Pull your shirt up."

Lauren was lying on her stomach and raised herself enough to lift her shirt to just below the shoulder blades.

"Higher."

Lauren pulled her shirt and the black sports bra beneath it to her shoulders, almost off. Jo then pulled the woman's shorts down, exposing the top third of her butt crack. Underneath was thong underwear that Jo also pushed down, just a bit. Jo studied the canvas. In the silence Lauren lifted her head for a moment and noticed pictures on the wall of two New England Patriot's football players. One she knew very well. The other she didn't recognize.

"Who's that?" Lauren asked.

The words were like a flashbulb in Jo's face, breaking her concentration.

Normally Jo ignored a customer's chattering, but this time grudgingly replied. "Tom Brady," referring to the photograph of the Patriot's quarterback, who inscribed the picture, "To Jo, a true artist, Tommy B."

"I know who *he* is. You know him? Does he have a tattoo?"

"I don't really know him. He doesn't have any tats that I know about–I did Nick's tat–see his left arm?"

Lauren examined the picture, hanging next to Tom Brady's, of a large man sporting on his forearm a muscular tiger, rippling with power, grace, balance, and speed. "Who is he?" she asked.

"Nick Glazier. He's the backup center for the Patriots," Jo informed her.

Keisha had posted the pictures for the draw Tom Brady provided, especially with the male clients. Though Jo never told anyone, it was the other player's inscription she cherished, "To Jo, an amazing athlete, Nick."

"Nick Glazier," Lauren turned it over in her mind.

Something in Jo's tone made her pry. "A friend of yours?"

"No," Jo snapped.

Jo was being only half truthful. She had met Nick once at Ink Angels and once after that. Since then he'd sent her several text messages asking to get together again. She liked Nick. Nick was a wonderful person. And that is why she would never see him again.

Jo wasn't in a chatty mood and changed the subject. "Put your head down and let's get this done."

Lying face down, Lauren relaxed her neck, still distracted by the photos. She bet there was a good story. One she wasn't going to hear. Jo looked at Lauren's back waiting for the design to come to her. The gym shorts half down distorted the woman's body. Jo ran her hand down her back and butt cheeks to get a read on the canvas she'd be working on. Her feel was like a doctor performing a routine exam. Lauren's expensive running shoes were worn as if they were used. The woman had a trim, athletic body and well-toned glutes. She was a runner and a serious one.

The tat on Lauren's ankle was a small, deep blue check mark representing a seagull in flight. She had waited until a breakup and then rushed to get this one done before another controlling male entered her life. She'd always lived up to another's expectations. The new tat was as much a statement as it was art. It would be bright and breezy. It was Deidra, not Lauren, who referred to it as a tramp stamp, so Jo knew that viewing this work was by invitation only. Jo designed it in her mind. She would position the tattoo so it could be visible when Lauren ran. It would be just at the belt line of her running shorts so Lauren could decide if it would be seen or not, depending on what she was wearing or how she wore it. It would beckon select future love interests, and, at the same time, say she was her own woman and could make her own decisions.

Spin the Plate

Jo ran her hand over the skin one more time to get a final reading on the texture and contours of the surface and to determine the size and placement of the image. It would be a single golden rose reflecting the sun's rays, blowing, but not bending, in the breeze. The petals would be subtly wind blown and the stem of the flower strong, supple.

"We have XM-Radio with over 200 stations," Jo remembered to offer.

"Here are the headphones and remote," she said as she handed Lauren the silencing device. "First I'm going to disinfect the area."

Keisha was out of earshot and Jo was eager to get started, so she skipped the detailed explanation each customer was required to receive. Jo had the spiel memorized by now: "There is a fairly long routine that needs to be performed before the artwork can begin. All over the skin are staph germs that we need to keep us alive because they kill germs that would otherwise hurt us. But if the skin is broken, those staph germs could turn toxic. So, the tattooed area needs to be surgically cleaned…" Blah, blah, blah.

Once a design fixed in Jo's mind, her fingers tingled to realize it.

"What's Nick like?" Lauren wondered out loud.

Boy, did Jo wish she'd be quiet. Jo was never verbose, but found conversation especially grating when she was working. Jo wanted to say Nick was a jerk, but he wasn't.

"He's okay," she responded reluctantly. "The skin lays better if you relax. Don't move. Don't talk."

As Jo shaved the lower back area she thought

about Nick for the first time in a long while. Jo was normally completely absorbed in her work. But Lauren mentioning Nick made memories of when she had first met him flood her mind.

The night certainly didn't start out like one that would change Jo's life forever. Around 9:30 pm, as Jo's last customer left the shop giggling with her friends and peeking into her pants at new turtledoves below her right hip, Keisha imperiously informed Jo that she needed to stay late. No explanations were offered. Jo's questions were rebuffed in the surly and tight-lipped fashion Keisha used when she was sitting on a secret and wouldn't budge. Jo fumed silently in the break room, flicking crumbs off the table with her fingers. She turned her gaze between a rerun of "The Fresh Prince of Bel-Air" blasting so Keshia could hear it from the other room and the slightly more engaging red second hand on the slowly ticking wall clock.

At ten past ten, the door chime sounded and the room was filled with enthusiastic greetings–booming male voices, two of them, and Keisha's happy shrieks of welcome. The sudden change of mood intrigued Jo enough to heave herself up from the table, click off the television, and round the corner for a look.

Keisha introduced Nick Glazier first, who came in to get a tattoo. His friend Tom Brady accompanied him. The reason they came at night, after hours, was that "Tommy," as Jo soon came to know him, attracted a crowd in the daylight. It was the price of fame and success.

Nick wanted a tattoo to celebrate the team's second Super Bowl win. Nick was an amazingly nimble 375 pounds and incredibly strong. As the backup center, his job was to call the offensive blocking scheme and to keep enormous men from tackling the quarterback. Nick told her he wanted something that represented power, strength, balance, and quickness. A cat quickly came to mind, but which was the right one?

Jo asked him why he wanted these qualities. She was asking out of pure professionalism, to design the tat. Jo had no idea her life would be altered with his response.

Nick began. "When I was in high school I was very, very big–already over 300 pounds, but not muscular. Kids used to push me around. My father was a sport's promoter, and on an extended summer trip to Japan he brought the whole family along. There, I was introduced to Takashi Soto, a Sumo wrestler. Takashi took an immediate liking to me and taught me about Sumo training. I thought these wrestlers were just fat, but they're extremely muscular. The big bellies are misleading. Their training is intense. I started Sumo exercises to improve my balance, endurance, and strength. I went from being just big and heavy to playing high school football, getting a scholarship at Georgia Tech, and eventually playing in the NFL. And, winning a Super Bowl."

Jo listened intently. She was just over 300 pounds herself at this point and though her size afforded her a certain protection from the world, the practicalities of living were becoming increasingly difficult. Stairs were a trial for her, walking any distance was a challenge, and jogging an impossibility. Worst of all,

Keisha was starting to take the more elaborate tattoo jobs herself and had even hesitated before giving Jo Nick's business.

"Tell me more," Jo said.

"Sure," Nick replied. "We fatties need to stick together."

Jo did not take the comment as an insult or a joke, but as it was intended–a statement of fact.

Nick went on. "Thousands of years ago, Sumo wrestlers would fight to the death, and even five or six hundred years ago, it was part of military training. Then, only the warrior class could fight Sumo. Now anyone who is prepared to work for years to become a Rikiski can do it. Training involves weight lifting, bicycling, jogging, yoga, and katas, which are a combination of wrestling moves and ballet. What Master Soto taught me, I use every day in my regimen. I owe my success to him."

Nick's tat was easy to design. A Japanese stylized tiger with the initials T and S in the stripes. When Nick's arm was still and hanging straight down, the tiger's head looked just slightly out of proportion, too big or maybe off-center for its body. But with the arm held in position for rushing at full speed toward an opponent, the tiger's head almost leapt off the arm in a 3 D effect. Jo began work on Nick's left arm, since, as Nick told her, the Patriots wouldn't allow a tattoo on the right arm due to the danger of infection or complications. Above the hum of the needles, Nick described to Jo the details of his training. She decided at that moment she wanted what he had.

At the halfway point, they stopped and ordered

take-out from a late night pizza place. When the hot pizza and subs arrived, they crammed into the break room.

Jo remembered how Nick pulled out her chair.

"May I?" he asked and looked her straight in the eye with a million-dollar smile.

This genuine gesture stirred a feeling that she wasn't used to and wasn't at all comfortable with. Reality and fantasy blurred. She knew with certainty that anyone with a penis was scum, dangerous, aberrant, predatory, evil. Yet, for a split second she allowed herself to acknowledge what she had been forcing herself to not think about: "boy is he good looking and polite and treating me so nicely." Unfamiliar emotions overwhelmed her.

Jo finished a couple of hours later. Keisha wanted to take a picture.

Nick apologized, but told her. "Mr. Kraft doesn't like us to take pictures, but I'll have the team photographer take one and send it to you."

Then he turned to Jo and said. "Actually, if you're serious about starting Sumo wrestling training, you can work out with me tomorrow morning."

Jo didn't know how to respond. Normally, she would reflexively respond no. But this was an amazing opportunity for her.

"My wife is a personal trainer, and I'm sure she'd be happy to help you," Nick offered.

"Wife?" thought Jo, noting Nick wore only his Super Bowl ring. She experienced a flash of disappointment. Then, relief. What was she thinking? Obviously, he was just being friendly.

"Yes," somehow tumbled from her mouth.

Nick wrote down the address, off of Newbury Street.

The next morning Jo arrived at the Harvard Club of Boston, which was elegant with copious polished mahogany. She asked the guard, who did not seem at all surprised to see a large woman in sweats, where to go. Nick was in the athletes' workout room. When Jo arrived she found not just Nick, but the entire Patriot's offensive line stretching out. These men were all heavier than her, and for once she felt like she fit in. She wasn't quite sure if that was a good thing.

There also were a few thin, fit, and gorgeous women working out who were wives and girlfriends of the players. Jo chose a spot near Nick.

Nick told her. "We have a private workout room so we aren't mobbed for autographs. Let me introduce you to my wife, Lindsay."

"You did an amazing job on Nick's tattoo," Lindsay said, at the same time giving Nick's arm a poke with her index finger.

"Ow!" Nick said reflexively.

"I thought you football players were supposed to be tough," Lindsay teased.

"I am," Nick said. "In a game."

Lindsay was a stunning woman. She was six feet two inches tall and had long, straight chestnut hair

Spin the Plate

caught up in a high ponytail. As the personal trainer her job was to facilitate the workout sessions. Jack McCreedy, the Patriots offensive line coach, was there with a chart and clipboard, but it was clear that Lindsay ran the show.

"Okay guys," Lindsay said. "Let's go. Five minutes."

All the men, each of them weighing in between 300 and 375 pounds, congregated in the ballet room.

Lindsay took Jo aside and asked. "What are your goals?"

Jo was dumbfounded. She didn't quite know how to answer.

"Was the walk here tiring?" Lindsay ventured.

That was an understatement.

"Well," Jo admitted. "I'd like to have an easier time climbing stairs."

Lindsay commented to Jo. "Offensive linemen need to be quick, strong, and have the endurance to play a three-hour game."

"That's what I want," Jo confirmed.

"Nick said you're interested in Sumo training. That'll help."

Lindsay continued. "Stick with me and we'll get you there. Let's go to the ballet room. Don't worry if you can't keep up. These guys have been doing this a long time."

Then Lindsay turned to face the group and said. "Okay everyone. Let's do this."

The ballet room at Harvard Club had a 25 foot square polished hardwood floor and a gleaming mirrored wall. First everyone stretched, using the wall-mounted bar for balance.

Lindsay called out yoga positions that everyone else seemed to know; then she'd quietly explain them to Jo.

"Just go as far as you can everyone." But this time by "everyone" she meant Jo.

The men partnered up, as did the girlfriends and wives, and Jo worked with Lindsay.

Lindsay said. "Okay. Let's go!"

Lindsay strode to the wall and hit a button. As music filled the room, Jo noticed the speakers high up on the walls. The Black Eyed Peas' "Boom Boom Pow" was the first song to blast from them. During the first hour they did kick boxing aerobics with Lindsay leading. Jo was impressed at how nimble these huge men were. Kicking. Punching. More kicking.

Jo was exhausted after about 15 minutes, but was determined to go on. At the half hour point everyone, except for Lindsay, was perspiring profusely. The pain consuming Jo's body was excruciating, but also exhilarating. The outpouring of sweat was not only a physical release, but an emotional one as well: frustration and anger, her constant companions, flowed from her. Despite the burning in her muscles, she felt almost content. At the 45 minute mark Lindsay saw Jo was staggering. Her eyes looked glazed. Lindsay took a break and handed Jo a bottle of room temperature water.

After several minutes, Lindsay clapped her hands together. "Okay, let's do it."

Then, to Jo. "Athletes need to have balance and strength. And great footwork. The next hour we're going to do ballet."

Jo was surprised to see how fluid the players' movements were. They were all wearing their blue sweatpants and sleeveless sweatshirts with the Patriot's logo on the front and their uniform numbers on the back. It was strange at first to see these men, most who weighed over 350 pounds and had bulging biceps, gracefully master ballet positions.

Jo attempted the various positions and gained confidence when she saw no one was mocking her. Nick showed her some tricks knowing big people had challenges. When she completed a near perfect arabesque, the men around her cheered a collective "Woo Hoo" and Nick smacked her palm in a spontaneous high five.

Jo had a taste of a something that she had never really known. Acceptance. It kind of scared her.

After the workout, Nick asked. "Can you join us for lunch?"

"Sure," Jo said. She was suddenly starving.

Jo went to the woman's locker room and was relieved to see individual dressing rooms with private showers. She found Lindsay waiting for her outside.

"Tired?" Lindsay asked.

"I can barely move," Jo admitted.

"Well, it gets easier. The guys have to do this five times a week. You're welcome to join us anytime. Here. Take my card. It has my cell number on it."

Jo didn't know what to say.

"Here we are," Lindsay said. "The Miller room."

They sat by large windows overlooking Newbury Street. The men ate massive quantities of food and had impeccable manners. They were out of their sweats now. Some had on shirts and ties, and others wore more casual button down shirts.

"Hey Jo. Come on over here," Nick invited.

Some of the other men, clearly impressed by Nick's tiger, wanted to hear of experiences she had as a tattoo artist. A couple were interested in her advice on body art that they were considering.

After everyone else had gone, Nick, Lindsay, and Jo continued chatting. Then, Nick reached under his seat and brought out two identical, rectangular packages. Both were loosely wrapped in bright white paper and secured by a single piece of scotch tape in the back.

The first one was a photo of Tom Brady with the inscription: "To Jo. A true artist. Tommy B."

The second was a photo of Nick with his new tattoo. "Mr. Kraft said it was okay to hang these up in the store, but asked you not to sell them or post them online."

"You didn't sign yours," Jo said.

Nick took a clip-on sharpie from inside his pocket, deftly pulled the photo from the frame, scribbled something, and slipped it back inside. He handed it to her.

The photo read: "To Jo. An amazing athlete."

"Okay," she replied, secretly pleased. "I'll give these both to Keisha, to hang up in the shop."

"Hold on," Nick said. "You know, I was impressed by your determination and strength."

He paused for a second and pulled a third package, larger but similarly wrapped, from beneath his chair.

Jo glanced at it and chewed her bottom lip.

"Open it. The only thing I ask is that you treat it as top secret. My teammates don't know about this. I may have to face them again."

Jo was apprehensive. Secrets and lies. She opened it tentatively. It was the training manual Takashi Soto gave to Nick when he was in high school.

"You're the only person besides Lindsay who's ever seen this. I called Soto's rep in Japan last night. He said it was okay to give it to you. So, here you go."

Jo leafed through the training manual. Everything they did that morning was there, plus a lot more. She snapped the handbook closed and stared at the gift, not daring to open the cover again. She longed to peruse the chapter list, but feared if she did she would be unable to refuse. She held it out to Nick.

"I can't accept this."

He looked relieved, but didn't reach for the book.

"Every word and illustration is committed to memory by now. I haven't even looked at it for years. Giving it to you, someone worthy of it, would be some major Karma. Still, I have to admit I'm having a hard time giving it up."

Jo continued to hold out the book, but inched the instruction manual slightly closer to her body.

Jo made it a habit not to consent to such offerings or the strings that invariably went with them. But Nick was enticing her with the Italian "magic three" interchange. It was ingrained in Jo from birth that even the most benign invitation of "Please take it" must be met with "No, really I couldn't." Perhaps in the old country this was a way of allowing people to be generous who had nothing to give away. But, after a third insistence it was permissible, and expected, to comply.

Then Nick proposed. "How about this. It's not a gift. Let's call it a loan instead. You can return it to me whenever you're done with it."

Nick took a business card out of his wallet and tucked it inside the front cover of the still slightly outstretched book. Only then did Jo draw the training manual to her chest.

"Okay."

A few minutes later, outside the Harvard Club standing at the curb, Nick asked Jo. "Can I give you a ride?"

"No. I'm all set."

Lindsay hugged her and told her what a great job she'd done. Jo stood stiffly, arms hanging down by her sides. With a smile and a wave, Nick and Lindsay pulled away in their BMW SUV.

Jo was physically spent, but the endorphins were still tingling within her veins and her brain buzzed. What a remarkable day. At that moment she felt accepted, wanted, liked.

She never went back.

She never saw Nick or Lindsay again, though she did trade text messages with Nick every now and then. For Jo, surviving in this life depended on her being a scowling, nasty bitch. Hanging around people, and especially these people, would change all of that, challenge her carefully crafted self image, and perhaps crumble it.

Men were scum, sick depraved bastards, no good

creeps, with ulterior motives rippling just under the surface. They were all evil; and the ones that seemingly started off nice were the very worst. Penises were weapons. Men were the real seducers–like Pandora's Box with a twist–luring women with their compliments and gifts, but eventually exposing all the evil of the world inside them. Women allowed men to be hateful so perhaps that made them even worse than men. Jo reflected on these truths constantly and wasn't about to stop now.

Then again, perhaps Nick Glazier, who proudly wore her tattoo, and his beautiful wife Lindsay were the hope in the box that humanity wasn't completely bad. All the same, Jo knew hope was one small step from trust, an open invitation to betrayal, and a most dangerous thing.

That afternoon, the return trip was different somehow. She was different. At home, Jo immediately began reading the manual. The next evening, she transformed her second bedroom into an exercise room. The next night her Sumo training began.

"How long will this take?" Lauren asked for the third time, pulling Jo back into the present.

"Ah…About an hour more," she said.

With the skin prepped, Jo was ready to get started. The first needle stick was always telling: whether a customer winced, teared up, or seemed not to notice. There would be hundreds of sticks and each more painful than the last. The needles were tiny and mounted on a special device that looked somewhat like a dental drill with the same low buzzing that muffled somewhat when the needles were sub-dermal. Jo had to be careful: lower back tattoos were on skin just millimeters above the lumbar vertebrae.

The first stick went well.

"Okay?" Jo asked.

"Good," was the response.

Jo immediately became absorbed in realizing the imagery that was in her head. A thin layer of sweat beaded on her upper lip; she breathed rhythmically. It was almost as though she was outside of her body watching each stroke appear on the skin replicating exactly her mental picture.

Now the tricky part of the tattoo was coming: the leaves. It would require precision artistry.

"Make sure to be very still during this part," Jo cautioned.

Lauren had forgotten how much getting a tattoo hurt.

"How much longer," Lauren asked, hoping for a small number.

"About a half hour more."

Thirty minutes later Lauren asked once again. "How much longer?"

"Just a few more seconds," Jo assured her. "And done. Do you want to take a look?"

Lauren couldn't wait. She jumped off the table planning to be in some pain, but was pleased when she didn't feel any. Lauren stood with her back to a full-length mirror and twisted her neck to get a glimpse as she waited for Jo to bring a hand mirror.

"Is it okay?" Lauren asked Jo.

Jo, with nondescript look on her face, responded. "It's good."

Spin the Plate

"Can I come in?" It was Deidra.

Deidra and Lakeisha joined them in the procedure room. Jo handed Lauren a mirror, which she took in her right hand, and with her left hand she pulled up her shirt. Her eyes widened. The rose blowing in the wind whispered yielding power. The gold showed its great value in the reflection of the sun.

"It's beautiful," Lauren whispered.

Lauren sounded choked up and her eyes were moist. This was not unusual. Often tears would spring to the customer's eyes or a smile would spread over the face. In any case, the person whose body now showcased Jo's art would fall silent and become still, spending some time taking in the work.

Lauren wanted to get a better look, so she took off her shirt. She was wearing a black sports bra. She then pushed her shorts down exposing the entire tattoo. She liked what she saw. She felt beautiful and desirable again.

Lakeisha had her camera out and was ready to take a photograph.

"I wanted to take a picture for the book. You probably want to put your shorts back on."

"Who sees the album?" Lauren asked.

"Anyone who comes in the store," Lakeisha informed her.

Lauren decided to not be the good girl she was always told to be.

"Get your camera ready," Lauren said. "Go ahead and take it."

Lauren added. "Just make it a close up!"

This was her first risqué photo shoot since the bear

skin rug shots at eight months of age. It made her feel unencumbered and free.

"I love it. Will it go in the book?"

"Only if you sign the waiver."

Keisha assured her. "If you change your mind I can always take it out later."

Lauren signed.

"Wait. Can you make me a copy?"

"Sure honey," Lakeisha said.

Lakeisha replaced one memory card with another and then inserted the original into a photo printer and hit "2." One copy went into the IA album and the other into a hidden pouch in Lauren's wallet.

"Oh, one more thing. Could I get a picture with Jo?" Lauren asked handing Keisha her cell phone.

Jo, as always, looked indifferent, but for now held off on the menacing.

After Lauren left, Jo cleaned up and prepared for her next client. She had four more appointments that day, three women and one man, plus she had some unscheduled blocks for walk-ins. Her next appointment was with a man named Murray, a regular. He told Jo to surprise him. She was planning a Japanese fan for his upper bicep with a rippling effect in the folds, which Jo knew would delight his grandchildren.

"The last appointment is at 7:00 tonight," Jo reminded Lakeisha.

"Okay," Lakeisha noted.

She didn't let on, but Lakeisha had known for weeks that tonight was special. It was the night of the Patriot's first pre-season game. Nick texted Jo several weeks ago confirming that he was scheduled to play with the starters for the first quarter. Jo didn't have a television at home. Lakeisha had installed a 32" plasma wall TV, which dominated the tiny break room and on which Lakeisha enjoyed watching snippets of soap operas, talk shows, and sitcoms between customers.

"The game starts at 8:00, doesn't it?" said Jo trying to sound casual.

"That's right sweetie," Keisha said and added with a mischievous smile. "I wouldn't miss it either."

Jo knew she was caught.

It was then Keisha divulged. "I'm locking up early tonight."

That evening Jo only half-followed the football's progression down the field. She spent most of her time watching the line play, keeping her eye on number 67 whenever Nick was on the field.

Jo didn't watch the game like the typical fan. She made no commentary, and her trademark scowl was always on her face. But, there was also a kind of calm. She'd look at these large, athletic men admiring their moves and strength and wondering what it would be like to be in the game. She was fairly certain with her power, speed, agility, and her seemingly endless endurance she could play professionally, if she were allowed. She reflected on getting paid millions for smashing into an opponent while massive cheers swelled from the crowds.

After the first quarter, Jo decided to go home.

CHAPTER 2: Dual Lives

At the same time, Francis Joseph Mangini was arriving to his home, a one-room apartment in the back of a small house in East Boston. He had just returned from his favorite haunt, the Three Aces Pizzeria. He did his best writing there. Plus, they let him order an item not on the menu: a basket of scali bread and butter.

His place was eclectic and minimalist. The walls were apartment white, with several pieces of art work, all originals and gifts from the artists. His favorite was made by an elephant named Sao, of the Phunket School. The multi-colored painting had long, gentle brushstrokes created by Sao holding a paintbrush in his trunk.

His other prized painting was by a Cape Cod artist, Steve Luecke, and was called "Dead Bee Behind a Beer Bottle." It showed a Coors bottle with a stiff insect feet-up that could be seen through the green glass, appearing even more true to life than a photo.

His office consisted of a desk purchased through Craig's List, a banker's light, a wireless modem, and a printer/scanner/copier/fax machine. The combination 12 inch TV and VCR on his desk was normally set to CNN, except when he flipped the channel to his one guilty pleasure: "American Idol." In this reality show, three music critics and the nation sifted through an ever dwindling pool of candidates to select the next up-and-coming pop singer.

The kitchen was merely a corner of his room with a small sink, a hot plate, and a college dorm room sized refrigerator holding a quart of milk, butter, and half a lemon. On top of the refrigerator were a loaf of Wonder Bread and a jar of peanut butter. The shelf above the sink held a stack of paper plates, a few cups, and assorted kitchen utensils.

His sleeping area was dominated by a double bed. Though he long ago decided to support the Franciscans in ways not involving direct membership, he hoped to have a permanent bedmate at some point in his life. For now, the comfy, oversized mattress provided more than enough room for just him. His dresser contained a seven day supply of underwear and socks, a pair of Levis, several T-shirts, and a couple of casual long sleeve shirts.

His closet was not so sparse. He had a tuxedo with tux shirts, tux ties, and cummerbunds; as well as five conservatively colored suits from Louis of Boston; three white dress shirts and three blue; a collection of mostly red, subtly patterned silk ties; two pairs of designer jeans and two pairs of pressed Khakis; a windbreaker for the fall and spring; and for winter a double-breasted camel hair topcoat and a North Face jacket. There was also a brown robe with a white rope belt, which he wore on a retreat one week a year.

He had four pairs of shoes, in addition to the worn Nikes he'd slipped off under the computer table. In a neat row in the back of the closet were shined tux shoes, black patent leather dress shoes, new Nikes, and brown Rockports.

His other space was a place no one else entered, or even knew existed: his one expression of vanity and hubris. Francis had contracted the build-out when the two women who owned the house were away on a five-day pilgrimage to Graceland in Memphis. A hidden sliding panel accessed this space where he went when he needed motivation, a reminder that his words mattered, things mattered. Proclamations, pictures, and articles plastered the walls of the tiny room crammed with high power computers and communications equipment. He would go there to do research, conduct business, recharge, and recuperate.

Sitting at his desk in the main room, Francis started up his computer and checked his email: three new messages from Charles Davis. Francis first opened one that had a subject line "Nice job on the speech." Then he checked the second message from Charles.

"Is Rome still on?"

Francis typed in "probably will know for sure by tomorrow."

Then he clicked "Reply."

Francis read the third message from Charles, "Went to Ernst and Young and got the check for tonight. All set."

Francis was distracted. He had been haunted all day by the woman he spoke to on the T. She was unlike any other woman he'd ever met: spirited, strong, iron-willed, absolutely unafraid. He closed his eyes and imagined the scowl melting from her face.

She looked serene. And beautiful. She was angry and hurting, but behind the hurt there was something there. He had to speak with her again.

He closed his email and did a Google search on IA in Massachusetts. Too many returns. Then he typed in "IA Boston Business Kecia." Nothing relevant. He tried "Kesha" instead, then "Keisha." Nothing. He entered just "IA Boston." Scrolling through the pages, he found six businesses within walking range of the Arlington T stop.

IA Interior Architects
Iranian Association
Independent Auto Repair
Italy and Beyond
IT Adventures
Ink Angels

Francis eyed the paneled wall across the room. He was tempted. He arose from his wooden chair, slid open the wall panel, punched in the combination, and slipped inside. Once barricaded within the hallway-sized room, Francis collapsed into a smooth green office chair and pushed a button on the side to convert it into a recliner. In that position it practically filled the floor space of the secret room. Francis pressed the back of his head into the supple leather and gazed at the facing wall covered with drawings he had sketched tacked on top of news stories, maps, calendars, agendas, and notes. The sketches were all of a warrior. A woman warrior. Some were close-ups, and below each eye was a rust-colored streak running all the way down her face.

Francis' eyelids were heavy. He closed them and

breathed in deeply. He was tired. He had the dream so often that he could see the image of this woman clearly, even in the drifting into sleep stage. He knew, as well as he knew anything, that she was real. And that she would save him. Her image brought raw pain of acute loneliness and with it deep longing.

Francis willed himself awake. He didn't have time for sleep. He glanced around him: a few minutes on the equipment, a few phone calls, and he'd have his answer. He reconsidered. And sighed. No. Engaging those resources for personal matters was strictly prohibited. He lingered for another minute then left his haven.

Back at his own, worn desk Francis glanced at the phone numbers and address listings on his personal computer and did a quick print. Tomorrow he would go searching.

"Please help me find her," he prayed.

It had been dark for hours by the time Jo made it back home to 614 California Avenue in Newton Corner, a mostly wealthy suburb of Boston. Jo lived in the working class section in a small apartment building with eight units. Hers was the basement apartment #1. The rent was expensive at $2,500 a month, but it was hard to find a complex that would allow the number of pets she kept.

Jo was welcomed first by Rufus, a Lab, Great

Dane, and Rottweiler mix. He was black with tan eyebrows and was enormous. Ben followed. He was all black except for a small spot of white on the chest and a few stray white hairs on his front toes. Ben was a Pit Bull, Greyhound mix and was tall and lean with a boxy skull and a powerful jaw.

Jo approached Rufus with her arms outstretched, and he greeted her back by launching his 120 pounds into them. His wagging extending from the tail to the second half of his body. Jo thumped the powerful dog to his delight. Then Jo turned her attention to Ben. She scratched his favorite spot, between his neck and shoulders, until he grunted in contentment. Next, Jo quickly checked on a small menagerie. Four pet rats were permanent residents. The rest were an ever changing assortment of temporary inhabitants: these were currently a ferret and three half-grown kittens.

She began her evening ritual by feeding the animals and taking the dogs outside to go to bathroom. Keeping busy was imperative. Jo knew if she didn't keep her focus elsewhere episode 62 would play to its finality, bringing memories and the accompanying pain that she was desperate to keep at bay.

All her animals had been picked up off the street, adopted from shelters, or received from people who brought them to her at the shop. Wild animals or ferals she would treat and later release. A pet animal would live with Jo until it was de-wormed, parasite free, restored to full health, and trusting enough to respond to another person. Then slipping the animal in the bib of her overalls or letting it follow at her heels, she would bring the creature to work with her to house in a cage Keisha let her keep tucked under a counter in the shop. It was not uncommon to see a furred face popping out from Jo's overall bib or a well behaved dog lying at her feet as she prepped a client. The animal would provided a comfort during the procedure–whether stroked by the customer before getting the tattoo or distracted by their antics from within the cage as the needles pierced the skin. Afterwards, many clients would leave with a new tattoo and a new pet.

After taking her dogs outside for a quick pee, Jo scooped kibble into their bowls and mixed in canned food. She was rewarded with a happy dog dance. No matter what her mood, her animals were thrilled to see her. She didn't know whether they should be admired or pitied for their questionable judge of character. As the dogs wolfed down their food, Jo headed for the rat cage.

Her four resident rattie boys stood up on hind legs all in a row and clutched the bars of the cage with tiny fists like four prisoners hoping for early parole. When Jo opened the top of the pen, Sammy, Muzzy, Jessie, and Jimbo came streaming over the sides.

Like most nights, tonight Ben and Rufus would accompany Jo as she traversed the city streets. As she snapped on the dogs' leashes, Jo admonished the rats, "Behave yourselves, use the litter box, and don't chew on the molding!"

Turning back to the dogs, she called out to them by their street names, "Titan! Cain!" which she used when they were out at night to help intimidate strangers. Rufus wriggled in delight and Ben waved his

Spin the Plate

powerful thin tail. They knew they were going into the city for the evening.

Jo scowled at them and said. "Hey. Toughen up!"

Titan's lip curled into a smile exposing his long white canine teeth, and Cain burst into an explosive series of barks.

"Okay, that's a little better," she conceded, though the tails were still beating the air.

"Let's go."

The three started out into the night. Jo had developed her own loping stride. She did not run or jog fearing a lean and thin runner's build would result. She moved in a rolling rapid gait bending her knees ever so slightly with a movement somewhere between a chimp on two feet and a Native American Ute hunter. In two hours, she could travel a 10 mile stretch from Newton to several of Boston's grimier neighborhoods, arriving there by midnight. She had never yet hit her limit in how long or far she could travel.

Ben was the tracker with a job to sniff and find. He was indiscriminate, seeming to be able to search and rescue any living creature, whether it was a rat in need, a cat, a dog, even a pigeon with a broken wing. Most of his finds were escaped or deserted pets of all sorts including reptiles, ferrets, bunnies, and the occasional gerbil. Ben kept his nose to the ground in one continuous sniff. Rufus held his head high, skipping along beside Ben, tail swishing back and forth. Ben's tail waved the air as he walked until finally, often behind a large green dumpster, he would tense his shoulder muscles, freeze, and stare intently.

Ben was always the first to find a creature, having

both the superior nose and concentration over the adolescent Rufus. Jo was never sure what species they'd encounter. So, she came armed with rolled oats, meat, an apple, baby food, and lactose-free milk for the animals. She carried packets of vanilla energy paste, too, which she consumed herself every 45 minutes for concentrated calories, protein, and potassium. These she would sometimes share with severely emaciated carnivores. Once Ben made a discovery, Jo listened to the sound of its movement and knew immediately the broad category, usually mammal but sometimes bird or reptile. Over time sounds would give away more information–size, weight, how low to the ground, number of legs, or in the case of a boa constrictor or other snake, no legs at all.

Certain animals were adept at street living, such as small colonies of feral cats. Jo kept an eye on them and intervened with medicines or food only when needed. She sometimes would have to trap a wild, injured animal, such as a squirrel. But she did not ever leave a trap unattended. Jo could very well imagine the vulnerability and panic a trapped animal felt and its awful fate should an ill-intended human or animal predator come across it.

Even though it was especially hard on Rufus, both dogs knew to sit quietly at a distance while Jo went to investigate a new discovery. If an animal was small, timid, or compliant enough she would retract him from hiding and tuck him into the bib of her overalls. Otherwise she would mentally mark the spot and return the next night alone or with just Ben to start the sometimes lengthy tame and capture process. Ben was

Spin the Plate

a help in drawing out dogs or puppies who saw humans as the enemy. Having him there sped the process. For adult cats or prey animals Jo would go at it alone.

The process required arduous concentration of maintaining immobility, regulated breathing, and a stream of barely audible sing-song encouragement. It might take days or even weeks of Jo wedged behind a dumpster having the animal learn her smell and the sound of her breathing, until finally she was granted the thrill of catching the first glimpse of a face peering out. Last week it was a half-grown black kitten with saucer-shaped yellow eyes, reluctant to come into the open and expose its vulnerability. The kitten finally emerged marching in place, moving a step forward, retreating a step back, afraid to come forward, too hungry to go back. She stared at Jo, hissed one final protest, and then resigned, with the pain of hunger outweighing the fear, she climbed onto Jo's lap into the open cave-like bib to be taken home.

When she roamed the streets, Jo was careful to avoid areas where the street kids hung out. She quickly took a detoured path if she unexpectedly spied a lone youngster or cluster up ahead. Whether the adolescents attempted to make friends or talked tough Jo felt the same longing to gather them up, like a litter of half-starved puppies without a mother, and bring them home. Seeing a girl out alone invoked an almost insatiable protective urge, a physical sensation that twisted and tore at her gut and made her chest throb painfully. Jo felt if she got too close, if she peered into the young girl's eyes, she would be unable to turn away. So she gave a wide berth to anyone out alone on the streets and short in stature.

Jo had learned this lesson the hard way. She had gotten too close, once. Since then Jo carried with her the haunting image of a slight girl with silky black hair and dark almond eyes and the worry over whether she was now okay or even alive.

It was almost a year ago. Jo had been out alone. As on most roaming nights back then, Jo's return trip in the wee hours of the morning loosely tracked the gaping gash that was the Massachusetts Turnpike. The Turnpike was noisy and unsightly, an eyesore whose rusting chain-link fences failed to keep its ugliness out of the neighborhoods, rich and poor, that it passed through.

Along the edges of the Pike, animals, the homeless, and other wanderers had built a network of paths and shelters, breaks in fences, camps, and exits out to the city streets. It was a miniature city of its own, with a street system and amenities for the desperate citizens of Boston only. Jo found it a convenient way to travel between the parts of town that had been separated by the highway, preferring it to the wide open bridges and avenues above.

On that night, Jo was about half way home, treading a path that for a few feet passed close to a cobblestoned courtyard on a dead end street. This was an expensive, gentrified section of the city, and, at 4 am, the hardworking residents of Bay Village were sleeping soundly, resting themselves to rise early and go earn the money for their hefty mortgages and Volvo leases. Just before Jo stepped into the clearing, she was startled by a soft, snuffling sound and low murmuring. She froze, just out of view of the street, bent low, and peered out carefully.

On the stoop of a classy townhouse stood a girl. Disheveled and sobbing, she adjusted her work clothes, which had clearly been put on hurriedly: stiletto heels, tight fitting black leggings, a tiny black miniskirt with belt, a low-cut leopard print top, and enormous hoop earrings. She pulled off a skewed wig of garish red hair. When the girl turned her face toward the street lamp, Jo realized in horror that this tiny prostitute was a child no more than thirteen or fourteen years old. A door slammed in the townhouse, and the sole light burning on the third floor switched off. The girl shivered as tears destroyed her makeup. Her muffled sobs were the only sound.

Jo was frozen in place, not wanting to reveal herself and unsure what to do, when headlights turned the corner of the short street.

"Shit," Jo mumbled as she watched a shiny black Lexus sedan glide to a stop right in front of the townhouse.

The girl made no move toward the car. The driver's side door opened and out stepped a man, medium sized, medium skin tone, unremarkable in every way except for the furious scowl on his face. He called out quietly but angrily to the girl in a guttural, choppy sounding language Jo did not recognize. The girl shook her head and replied, pointing to the third floor window. The trick had ended badly, apparently. The man's voice rose; he gestured angrily toward the passenger door. The girl shook her head again, and the man bounded up the steps.

He seized the girl by the hair with one hand, covered her mouth to muffle her cry with the other, and dragged her down the steps to the sidewalk. On the sidewalk, he swung her around with his back facing Jo and persisted in his incomprehensible grilling. Then, he raised his hand to strike her. But to his surprise, an iron hand wrapped around his wrist, a granite shoulder came up under his side, and he went crashing down onto the hood of a parked car.

The girl gasped and backed away as Jo seized the man again. He never saw or heard her coming. As he tried to right himself on the car hood, Jo smashed her fist into his upturned face. Blood and spit sprayed out; a tooth hung crookedly in his gaping mouth. His hands shot toward her but she already had a handful of his hair and one forearm. She flipped him over like a pancake and smashed his face again into the hood of the car. The car alarm started its rant. In one smooth move, Jo tossed the man off the hood like cheap baggage. He hit the sidewalk face first and emanated a soft groan. Jo stepped gracefully between his spread-eagled legs and aimed a field-goal kick directly between them. He let out a shriek and vomit flowed from of his mouth, puddling around his face. He lay still.

"Fucking pimp," Jo spat at him.

The car alarm had stopped honking, but a light was on in the townhouse. Jo looked the girl calmly in the eyes. Obviously this victim was not, as Jo wished for a flickering instant, one she could slip into her overall bib. Jo would never forget the look in the girl's eyes; she saw in them the terror, abuse, and shame of the years, with just the tiniest hint of relief beginning to creep in.

"Run," Jo said.

The girl spoke enough English to understand the word and what this moment meant to her. She pivoted and leapt away like a gazelle. With a quick tip tapping on the cobblestone, the girl vanished into the darkness. Then, Jo disappeared through a hole in the fence to the litter-strewn highway.

Jo never took that route again.

Now, tonight, at 3:40 am, after hours of tracking with no success, the night sky began to lift from pitch-black to charcoal. Time to go home. Jo called the dogs, and the three headed back. At the apartment, Jo closed the tired canines in her bedroom. Then, she went in search of the rattie boys. Sleepy from a night at play, all four were holed up, napping. They were nowhere in sight. Jo toasted bread and smeared on some peanut butter.

"Come-come-come," she called.

One by one rat heads emerged out of hiding, from behind a book shelf and under a clothes pile. The rats stretched and yawned exposing long incisors that they tucked away as they scampered towards Jo crawling up the denim on her legs. They grabbed greedily for the rat delicacy. She slipped them back into their pen. Each boy raced to a private spot to gulp down and protect his morsel.

The rats, when caged, lived in the spare bedroom. Jo's apartment had two bedrooms, a tiny kitchen opening into a living room/dining room combo, a full bath, and a half bath. One room was her bedroom which she shared with the dogs and the second was her workout and animal rescue room. In the spare bedroom one wall was lined with cages. Otherwise, it mimicked the Harvard Club layout complete with mirrored wall and stretching bar. It contained a rowing machine, Nautilus, yoga mats, and a treadmill. On a side table was the worn copy of the Sumo wrestling manual that Nick loaned to her.

After feeding the residents and donning sweat pants, sneakers, and an oversized T-shirt, she stretched and then warmed up with 10-pound weights. Now the real workout began. She was tired by this point in her day. She had to make sure the workout was rigorous enough to keep mind and body fully engaged and to prevent triggering an episode.

In her basement quarters she had no worries of bothering the neighbors. Five miles on the bike. Two miles on the treadmill set at ten minute miles at four percent incline. More stretching. Then she progressed to the weights. She bench pressed her weight: 260 pounds. Ten reps. Then curls, military press, leg lifts.

Now the mood shifted. She put on Aaron Copeland's Third symphony, slipped off her sneakers, and in stocking feet danced for 20 minutes. Graceful. Strong. Athletic.

By 6:00 am, Jo was completely spent. She slipped off soaked sweats and donned an oversized flannel nightshirt. She'd shower later. This morning, like every other early morning, she fell into a dreamless, exhausted sleep, knowing she would not stir until the radio alarm blasted four and a half hours later. "Around and around we go" was her final thought as she drifted off. Today, tonight, tomorrow, and yesterday all merged into one predictable, comfortable routine.

CHAPTER 3: First Date

Later that morning, suddenly and without warning, the routine unraveled. On this morning, the alarm did not blast. Instead, at 10:30 am the radio alarm clicked on and between-the-stations static hummed. Jo slept. Thirty minutes later her eyeballs shifted rapidly under the lids. She began to stir and then to thrash.

Episode 62 played in her head: *"The Dollhouse." This one starts out with a little girl sitting on her bed combing light caramel curls with a cherrywood-handled brush and comb and mirror set her Daddy had given her last week. She pulls down a banana curl with the brush and watches it bounce back up in the hand mirror. She examines her face critically, looking hard into her chocolate brown eyes framed by long lashes. She looks up from the mirror as Daddy strolls into her bedroom with a huge and bright pink dollhouse stretched across his open arms, turning to balance it on one arm and a knee, locking the door behind him. A moment later, Mommy raps on the door and says Juliana are you in there? He bellows at the closed door Do you want me to come out! And Mommy scurries away. As he turns back around, a scowl melts into an excited grin. He sits on the floor and shows her all the features; see the closet door and the little dresser drawers that really open. She hopes faintly that he's come to play dolls with her. He says to her Daddy has given you a wonderful gift... and now it's time for you to give him a little something. No Daddy, No Daddy. Come on darling, you know I'll take it slow. I'm always gentle. I have some special oil and I'll tickle you for a long time first. No, Daddy, she whispers. Fine! I don't have time for this shit. He grabs her and tosses her over his lap face down, flips up her dress, jerking down white panties. He grabs the cherrywood handled brush lying on the bed and smacks her bare butt. She cries out and squeezes her eyes shut and tries to lie very still, but feels him fumbling for his fly and knows he is pulling out a fat pink penis. He moves into a rhythm smack, pull, smack, pull and moans as the warm sticky stuff spurts onto her side. He stands abruptly and she falls, crumpling to the floor. His face red, he sputters, I work my ass off for this family, give them everything, and ask for so little. And I get shit in return. He grabs up the dollhouse in one hand and stomps out of the room. She knows not to come out and hides under the bed covers with a forefinger pressed into each ear.*

The next morning she feels stiff and sore. Her Mommy is cross with her jaw red and swelled up. She shakes the fruit loops into Juliana's bowl and says why can't you just cooperate and be a good girl? She chews on a fruit loop slowly, staring at the kitchen clock as the number flips from 8:12 to 8:13. She steals a sideways glance at the dollhouse in the corner of the kitchen. At 8:14 Mommy puts it outside on the curb. And, at 8:17 through the kitchen screen door she sees the dirty army-green trash truck pull up, and the trash man toss her lovely pink doll house into the back, and pull away.

At the sound of her ringtone, Jo's eyes flew open. She fumbled for the phone, flipped it open, and looked down to see "Dad cell" on the screen.

She answered it. "What do you want? You sick fuck."

He replied. "Come on now."

He paused, then continued. "Uncle Gino is turning 80, and Victoria's having a big ta-do over at Anthony's."

No response.

"Your mother wants you to be there."

She snorted. "Not a chance in hell."

"Okay, well you remember where the restaurant is, on Canal Street right there off of Charles. It's next Sunday at 2:00."

Jo hung up.

It was then that the time on her cell phone registered. 11:03.

"Shit!"

Still, right now she needed a shower. She took a moment to bring the dogs outside and begged them to pee quickly. Back inside she turned on the shower and stood under the stream. As the water changed from cool to scalding hot she scrubbed off the top layers of skin with Irish Spring soap. She tilted her head up toward the showerhead, eyes closed, letting the water hit just below her lower lashes and roll down her cheeks.

Jo thought. "Today is the day where it all falls

apart. Where I can't do it anymore. Where I don't make it."

The water continued to sting and burn her body.

Suddenly, she gulped a deep breath like someone rescued from drowning and decided. "No. I can do this."

She snapped off the water, stepped out of the shower, and with brisk swipes rubbed herself semi-dry. She threw on her clothes and bolted for the train.

Even though she was late, again, she never liked to take the same train or the same car two days in a row, preferring the increased chance of conflict with fresh meat. Today, especially, she was in the mood for a fight, or at least a decent altercation. Scanning the crowd she half-noticed the scrawny man who had sat across from her yesterday, absorbed in a newspaper. The 12:17 rolled in and figuring she was late anyways, she purposefully missed it and waited on the 12:24.

Francis sat through the pulling in and pulling out of the first train and boarded the second. He walked down the length of the cars and trailed her onto the second to the last one. Jo found a seat, and he settled directly across from her. She scanned the car, alert and as always eager for any potential trouble. She relaxed in disappointment as it seemed everyone was preoccupied in his own little world or was staring blankly out a train window.

She turned her attention half-heartedly to the man who she recognized from the day before sitting across the aisle. He looked to be youthful, but not young. When her gaze focused straight ahead she was caught off guard to see the little man staring intently back into her face.

He found her.

"That was easy," Francis thought, surprised. He'd been tracking her the past several months marking the sightings on his hidden room wall-map with colored pushpins, each with a time and date label. The only discernable pattern was that she never took the same mode of transportation two days in a row. Until today.

He wondered where she was going, where she worked. Not wanting to seem like a stalker, he slipped his "IA" Google search printed pages out of sight, praying for something to say.

"Jesus knows all the good you're doing."

Sometimes, as inconvenient as it generally was, Francis received "a word" and felt obliged to pass it along. She shook her head back and forth slowly a few times eying him and made no reply.

When she emerged from the train, the little man followed scampering at her heels, taking three steps to her two. She headed for the park, secretly thankful for the distraction he provided. Jo was not at all sure she could handle another episode today.

Francis felt an unfamiliar nervousness and compensated with rapid fire questions. "Where do you work? Have you always lived in the city? Do you like empanadas?"

She mostly ignored him, except for occasionally punctuating the conversation with, "You are a crazy fuck."

When they arrived at Ink Angels, Francis thought. "Didn't see that."

Jo didn't wear any tattoos, at least none he could

see. All tattoo artists he knew, from reality TV, were covered.

Arriving at the shop, Jo wordlessly grasped the shop door handle.

"Oh, you work here," Francis commented, then practically shouted. "Wait!"

She hesitated, just long enough for him to blurt out. "Can I take you to dinner?"

In the pause that followed he interjected. "You gotta eat."

Jo was shocked to hear herself reply. "What the fuck. Meet me outside after work on Saturday."

She disappeared through the door before saying a time. Francis checked the hours posted outside the door. The sign read "Saturday 1 PM - 10 PM." He didn't know when she got out. Decision time. Did he go inside to ask and chance her having second thoughts or did he assume 6:00 maybe 7:00 o'clock? That's dinnertime, after all. Better yet, he would arrive before 6:00 and wait for her to get off work.

Francis thought better of pursuing Jo into her sanctuary. He'd already risked lingering outside the door too long. Before she had the opportunity to renege, he melted into the sidewalk traffic and was gone.

Francis returned Saturday evening at 5:47 pm. He leaned against the brick wall several feet from the front door of the shop and scanned the face of each exiting person. He paid particular attention on the hour and half hour. Six o'clock came and went. Nothing. Same thing at 6:30. At 7:05, he pulled on the hood of his sweat shirt and slid down the wall hugging his knees with his head tilted to the right, eying the door.

By this time the sick feeling in his stomach and the pounding in his chest with each bell ring as the door opened and closed had subsided enough for him to start feeling bored.

"I'm so bored," he thought to himself.

In his back pocket he had a New Testament and a credit card-thin PDA which was as powerful as most laptop computers. He had a speech he needed to finish. He'd been up since 4 in the morning writing it. He decided he'd had enough of work for one day and besides he didn't want to draw attention to himself to passersby. More importantly he wasn't ready to risk having to explain to Jo, yet, why he carried a $5,000 Personal Digital Assistant in the back pocket of jeans that were just a few wears away from a hole in the left knee.

He was itching to pull out the New Testament though. For Francis, theology, rather than being a set of facts to be memorized and then vehemently defended, was more like an intellectual and spiritual video game. Reaching one level of enlightenment excited him briefly, but ultimately only increased his hunger, driving him into pursuit for the next level.

He was reluctant to have Jo catch him absorbed in the Bible.

"Enough with the pushing-Jesus," Francis thought.

He immediately wondered if such a thought was sinful and decided it probably was.

So he mouthed silently. "Lord God, forgive me."

Then he went on. "You know, if this works out I think it would be a good thing for me. And for You, for us both. Help me. Let me know what to say, what to do. Let it not end with tonight. Open a door for me. Please?"

Francis resisted the urge to check on the scriptural writings about healing, helping, and the second coming for an idea he was working through. Because, other than during the annual Franciscan-style retreat, he had no one with whom to discuss or debate such topics, he liked to engage in an internal dialog, taking the two sides of the argument.

"Do you think Jesus is a woman?" he asked himself now. "Self, I know, I know, in the first coming He took the shape of a man, but think about it. If you read all firsthand accounts of His work, what was He doing? He was healing, helping out, serving, even bathing feet. He was pretty much constantly trying to talk some sense into people, persuading them to get along better. If I read the Bible to someone who never heard it before and used a gender neutral name, like Chris, and said at the end describe 'Chris' I bet the person would just assume a woman. Of course it wasn't practical for Him to come as a woman on round one. He would have been stoned on the spot. Do you think in the second coming when Jesus bursts through the clouds on a chariot of white horses we'll see a woman with long chestnut hair flowing behind? Well, maybe this whole distinction is bogus, the gender thing

I mean. It could be another of those artificial distinctions we use on earth to make ourselves feel superior to one another."

Francis was becoming excited about the path this idea was taking, but he cut off the progression anyway knowing that he couldn't commit any more ideas to memory. The train of thought would be lost without jotting down a few notes or making a diagram. He knew he would be unbelievably frustrated with himself to reach a new height and then later be unable to recall exactly what it was.

By now it was almost 7:30 and still no sign of Jo.

Francis heard the Ink Angels' door chime and looked with anticipation, hoping it would be Jo. Nope. It was a man about 40, thin, tall with long blond just starting to gray hair in a pony tail and a brand new tattoo on his forearm. He came out of the shop, admiring the new addition to his body: a rider-less motorcycle clearing a jump with its engine in flames. He revved a Honda CRF on-and-off road bike and zoomed away.

Francis kept a keen eye on the door, but no Jo. He looked at his watch again–7:47. Hunger pangs started brewing. He briefly considered pulling out the condiment container of Jif creamy peanut butter from his sweatshirt pocket. But knew he might need something if the restaurant served only organic, fancy, or ethnic food. 8:12, back to thinking about the speech. What he wouldn't do for a pen and a scrap of paper.

Quick look at the watch–8:23. Starving and bored.

Francis wanted to continue on the speech, but his brain was fried. At 8:35 still no Jo. He knew he'd be able to hear the opening door chime, so he thought he would close his eyes for second. At 9:05 the door chime rang–Francis bolted awake. Not Jo. Now his back hurt.

Some time later he lay down, curled in a ball, resting his back against the wall. Struggling to stay alert he focused his attention on a young girl leaving the shop, alone. She had straight dark hair, low ride jeans, and sad eyes. Though the evening was cool the girl wore just a tank top with strings tied in the back. She walked with her head turned to the side, eyes fixated on her left shoulder at an enormous butterfly in an array of vivid blues. From Francis' vantage point it appeared to be about to lift off her shoulder, its wings fluttering a message. Francis strained to hear it. Yes, of course. "Freedom."

Francis closed his eyes. At 10:12 pm, Jo nudged him awake with her foot.

"Ready?"

He leapt to his feet and glancing down noticed a partially crumbled dollar bill and some change on the ground. Jo noted the adroitness with which he flipped up the coins and guessed that begging was likely the source of his livelihood.

He smiled and said. "Oh good, the tip."

Jo wondered if he was homeless.

"How long have you been sitting here for?" Jo asked him.

"For a while. I forgot to ask you when you got out of work," Francis confessed.

"Why didn't you just come in?"

"I don't know. I didn't want to bother you."

"Are you strange or something?" Jo asked.

"Kind of, but in a good way," assured Francis. "Hey, are you hungry?"

"Yeah," said Jo. "There's a diner near my house that's open 24 hours. They have homemade Twinkies."

Francis was intrigued by the thought, but not enough so to augment his short list of safe foods.

"Sounds good. Where do you live?"

"Newton Corner. I have to let my dogs out, first," she said. And added. "Hurry or we'll miss the last bus."

They had to run the final half block to the stop to reach the waiting bus. The driver, who recognized Jo as a regular on her route, held the doors.

On the ride Jo clarified. "Okay. By the way, if you think this is a date, it's not. For it to be a date, there needs to be kissing or the possibility of getting laid, and you're not getting a fucking thing."

"I didn't know there were rules," said Francis.

"Well, there are," Jo stated.

Francis was disappointed that there wouldn't be kissing, but secretly relieved that the pressure was off as far as trying to figure out when, where, and how much to romance Jo.

"Any other rules I should know about," Francis asked only half joking.

"Plenty, but we can cover them as we go," said Jo.

Francis liked the long-term sound of that.

Jo continued. "Not really a rule, but I'm not much for small talk." Other than television sitcoms, there was nothing like inane dribble to set Jo's mind wandering.

She continued. "And I never find quiet awkward."

They rode the rest of the bus ride in silence looking out the window. The bus dropped them off about 12 blocks from Jo's apartment.

"So, do you like being a tattoo artist?"

"Today was a good day. I had a Bohemian guy come in and I did his forearm."

"I know. I saw it. It was very colorful, with the orange and blue flames."

"I finished that one at 7:30. You were waiting that long?"

"Well, I got some stuff done," he said.

"And then I did a girl's entire left shoulder. You saw her leave about 9:30. After that I just sat there thinking you stood me up. I didn't realize I'd have to go out and search for you."

"Sorry about that," Francis said apologetically; but at the same time he was happy to know she not only waited for him, but waited long enough to practically miss her bus.

Jo disappeared into her basement apartment and reemerged led by one large and one enormous dog, both rippling with muscles under tight skin and short black fur.

"Hey Buddies," Francis said to them.

They briefly greeted him, and then the dogs went right to business marking favorite sign posts and relieving themselves. Francis' calm demeanor and the animals' response to him earned him a few points with Jo.

The dogs strained to continue down the street but Jo pulled them back into the apartment and told them sternly. "Wait a while."

She and Francis walked down to the Blue Arrow Diner on the corner of Washington and Cleveland streets. The Blue Arrow had bar-style seating with attached, padded stools just outside the kitchen. There were four small booths against the walls on either side and long tables with benches in between. Along the walls were chalkboards with the menu and specials written on them in colored chalk.

A woman in her 60's with a faded name tag that read "Terry" greeted them. "Table for two?"

"Yes, please," Francis answered.

Francis read the walls and menu twice and rested the closed menu on the table for some time before Terry, the host/waitress/cashier, returned to their booth.

"What would you like?" she asked.

"I'll have the lumberjack breakfast with a side of corn beef hash," Jo said.

"I'll have an English Muffin, toasted with peanut butter," Francis said.

The waitress said. "We grill them. It's very good."

Jo thought Francis looked pained. Francis' mind flooded with images of the assortment of food items that had touched the grill in the previous day or perhaps days with only the scrape of a spatula between each for a cleaning.

He asked. "Is there any way you could toast it?"

"Sure," Terry said scribbling on her pad.

"To drink?" Terry asked.

"Chocolate milkshake," Jo said.

"Water is good. With lemon please," Francis replied, handing Terry the two menus.

"I thought you were starving?" Jo said.

"I am," he replied.

Jo's milkshake arrived along with Francis' water. He mixed seven packs of sugar into the lemon water.

Jo's oversized plate held 3 pancakes, 3 pieces of French toast, 3 strips of bacon, 3 sausage links, and scrambled eggs. There was a heaping bowl of homemade corned beef on the side with freshly grated and fried hash browns mixed in.

Francis' plate had two sides of a toasted English muffin with peanut butter on them. He sighed in relief to see it without any grill marks.

"I've lived in East Boston my whole life," Francis ventured. Jo looked nonplused. "My two aunts raised me." Mild interest.

He continued on. "My parents... I never got to know them, not really. They died when I was three."

Now he had Jo's full attention. He could see she really wasn't the small talk type.

So he explained. "They were on their way to an office Christmas party one evening, when a newly licensed 16 year old girl, heavily pierced and with a car full of friends, didn't realize her street came to an end at a T in the road, and barreled into my parents' car nearly head on. Their car spun out and slammed into a stone wall, releasing its fluids and airbags. My parents were okay though. They had just stepped out of the car to phone from a nearby house when a flat bed truck coming around the curve from the other direction plowed into them both. My father died at the scene. My mother was in a coma. I guess there were a lot of tubes and bandages, I don't remember visiting her in the hospital. She never gained consciousness and after a couple of weeks she passed on, too."

"Can I get you anything else?" Terry asked.

Francis looked across the booth at Jo who said, "I need to feed the dogs."

"The check and four homemade Twinkies. Two to go," Francis said.

He explained to Jo. "For my aunts."

"You see your family willingly," Jo commented. "I do the family thing once a year. My sentence is tomorrow. It's going to take me all morning to get across town to Malden thanks to the cuts in weekend T and bus services."

Francis hoped this was his open door and quickly asked. "Tomorrow…can I drive you?"

The homemade Twinkies arrived, still warm. They were heaven, Jo thought. Best she'd ever had.

Francis declined. "No, thanks." And said. "Please, go ahead," nodding toward the Twinkie still on the plate, when Jo asked if he was going to try one.

Francis was thankful that she didn't pry about his limited diet which was remarkably similar to his menu at the time of his parent's death.

When he was reasonably certain Jo's mouth was emptied of the creamy goodness, he said. "You didn't answer me."

"Fine. Pick me up at 1:00."

They walked back. It was a crisp, but not cold, late-September night.

With the sound of Jo's approaching footsteps Rufus began to howl, and Francis said. "I can hear your dogs barking to see you, so I'll let you get going.

I had a nice non-date and I'll see you tomorrow."

Francis hoped Jo assumed he was taking a cab. Even though he had enough money left over from dinner, a taxi ride home would have been a budget buster. He had parked his car a couple of streets over earlier that day and used his Charlie Transit pass to get to Ink Angels from there. Since she didn't ask about the taxi, technically it wasn't a lie. Though, he supposed the faked phone call he had made to "pick me up at the corner of California and Washington" was pushing it.

As Jo walked into her apartment, she half regretted giving him a second non-date date, but he'd stirred her curiosity. The thought was broken by the plaintiff wail of dogs that were used to getting fed at ten thirty, not midnight. Jo arrived inside to an enthusiastic greeting and began the feeding ritual.

While the dogs wolfed down their dinner, she mused. "What a weird little freak."

CHAPTER 4: Meet the Parents

The next day Jo was sitting on the cement stoop in front of her apartment when Francis pulled up driving a nondescript green Chevy Nova. He had actually arrived 45 minutes earlier and had been circling the neighborhoods. Even though it was Sunday, he was apprehensive about maneuvering through Boston traffic and the thought of getting lost on a route he'd only taken once before. He jumped out of the car to meet her.

He noticed her gaze and asked. "Like the wheels? The car was a high school graduation hand-me-down present from my aunts."

Francis continued. "That and a two and half ounce bottle of Jake cologne which I still have by the way. I save it for very special occasions."

In the early fall breeze Jo noted that he smelled nice.

Francis admitted. "I really don't drive much."

Jo, with a hand on the passenger-side door handle, glanced through the window at the odometer noting that it read only 78,303 miles.

"Anthony's is across the city," Jo said

"Do you drive? Do you want to?" Francis asked her.

Spin the Plate

She shrugged. "Sure," and walked around to the driver's seat.

On the drive, Francis ventured. "So, we'll be seeing your folks."

Jo made no response.

Francis asked. "Tell me about them."

Jo evaded. "Nothing much to say. A pretty boring pair, actually."

Francis was in the habit of learning about people before he met them, especially when he wanted to make a good impression.

He pressed. "Really, I want to know."

Jo launched into a reply. She planned to start with a few dates and facts and then wrap it up quickly with a general, sweeping statement.

Jo began, "My mother married late, especially for those days. My father to this day enjoys reminding her that he was 'her last chance' as though she still owes him. I was born a few months after she turned 40."

Once she got started, Jo realized how long it had been since she'd said any of this out loud; there had been bad results in the past. It felt good to let the words spill out.

"What the hell," she thought. "He asked."

Jo kept her eyes focused on the road ahead. She related the events like a news report of a flash flood, bombing, or other disaster. The account was factual and impartial, providing play-by-play detail of the unfolding drama. She started with her earliest childhood memory. She had just turned three years old and had an elaborate birthday party with pony rides in the back yard. It started getting dark and everyone went home. Her mother was downstairs cleaning up. She was playing in her bedroom with her new puppet theater when her father came in and told her about "a puppet in his pants." She remembered him pulling out a pink thing that looked to her then like the neck of her Nana's Thanksgiving turkey. He chased her in the bedroom with the pants puppet, poked it at her, and tickled her. She laughed hard and had a queasy feeling in her stomach.

Jo said. "It escalated from there."

With the floodgates opened, Jo walked through the events chronologically, maintaining the news reporter tone, hitting the essential facts and the firsts: the first time he exposed himself, first penis-vaginal contact, first penetration, and at seven, first orgasm inside of her.

"It was pretty much a monthly episode," she said. "Until I left the house for juvenile hall at 14."

Though shaken, Francis could see Jo was not finished telling.

"Juvenile Hall?" he repeated, inviting her to continue.

"Now, that is a whole other story," she said. "My parents bought me only dresses and a lot of sweaters, which by 8th grade were getting tight. I was taller than the other girls and my curves came in early. Boys were attentive and some liked to fiddle with me behind the school, feeling my breasts. I didn't mind. One boy went too far and put his hands under the skirt of my dress. When I pushed his hand away, he shoved me down and laid his body on top of mine. I grabbed his wrist, pushed, twisted, and heard a snap. The boy turned white. I felt bad; I didn't mean to do that. I let him fuck me to say I was sorry. And, to keep him quiet. He would have too, except apparently he was on some Olympic development team; who even knew they had lacrosse in the Olympics? He didn't tell right away. But eventually his dad punched it out of him. When the detective came to the school to question me, he discovered that I'd taken to carrying my dad's handgun in my backpack. That, along with the fact that the judge was a good friend of a friend of the boy's father, well, I spent almost two years in juvi."

She told Francis that the time in juvenile hall was the best part of childhood, such as it was. First of all it got her away from him. Second she learned how to protect herself and picked up the necessary survival skills for not only the present circumstance, but also to prepare for any future prison time, and life itself.

She quipped. "The wisdoms I picked up there would make for a pocket-sized book to sell at the front counter of Barnes and Noble, 'All I Really Need to Know I Learned in Juvenile Hall.'"

It was there Jo discovered the top three ways to deflect a beating and, when necessary, how to take one without crying out. She learned to show no emotion except disinterest and menace: heavy on the former with those in power and on the latter with everyone else. There she came to realize that ultimate control comes from not giving a damn about anything, or anyone, and most especially yourself.

There was nearly unlimited weight room access. The gym was one of the few places consuming enough to keep her mind from wandering back to episodes perpetrated by her father. Frequent workouts plus a steady fare of bologna, baked beans, and cling peach halves in heavy syrup rocketed her weight from 145 to a solid 250. As her body transformed she experienced with it, for the first time, a surge of power. She was awarded a wider berth and begrudging respect from the other girls and an increasing disinterest from the male "chaperones." Chopping her hair into a ragged bob and dying it black with contraband shoe polish completed the effect.

Jo's one big mistake was that she did not foresee that an unwanted side effect of her under-the-radar approach would be early release for good behavior. Three months before her 16th birthday, she was handed off to her parents with an ankle tracking bracelet and court order for house parole. Both parents retrieved her as both were required to be present and sign the release forms.

Once the three were alone in the car, her father greeted her with, "You look like shit."

She responded. "What do you care, you sick fuck." and braced herself for a heavy back handed slap across the face.

None came.

Her father gripped the steering wheel tighter. They rode in silence, with her mother rubbing the palm of one hand over the knuckles of the other the whole way home.

And with that, as suddenly as it had started, the episodes were over.

Francis was silent in the seat next to her. Jo wasn't sure he was listening. Maybe like the few others she'd told when she was younger, he had rolled up an invisible glass window between them in denial, distaste, disgust, *horror.* Maybe he'd fallen asleep. Well fuck him. She was driving so she would certainly get to the restaurant. She didn't much care if he took off from there and she never saw him again.

Jo risked a quick sidelong glance. She saw Francis with tears flowing unabashed, feeling fully the fear, pain, and shame of the young girl with golden curls and deep, brooding brown eyes.

Francis wiped his eyes several times, and they continued on their way to meet Jo's family. They drove without speaking, neither knowing what to say or do next. Francis was overwhelmed as he attempted somehow to process the sadness, pain, and injustice that was Jo's childhood.

Jo's mind raced trying to fathom why Francis appeared to be so moved. Why would he care about her? He barely knew her. Maybe his reaction was a ploy. An attempt to score some points–erroneously thinking he could cash in later. Jo was about to call him out with a stinging accusation. But she held back. Something inside her couldn't help but notice the authenticity of his quiet tears.

Suddenly, Francis brightened with an idea.

"I know where we are," he piped up. "Let's stop and meet my aunts. It's right on the way."

He added. "If you aren't in a rush to get to the party."

After a pause, Jo responded. "Fine."

"Francis, what a wonderful surprise!" two stout aunts shrieked, as they descended upon Jo with open arms.

Jo disappeared, from the neck down, into ample bosoms and warm, fleshy hugs. They introduced themselves as Francesca and Angelina, but Jo didn't catch which was which.

Stepping back Aunt 1 threw her hands up and exclaimed. "Just look at you!"

Aunt 2 said to Francis. "She's lovely, just like you said."

Aunt 1 continued. "So pleased to finally meet you."

Aunt 2 finished. "We've heard so much about you."

The exuberance of their greeting made Jo curious as to the attention bestowed on a woman who actually had *completed* a second date with their nephew.

"Come, please sit down," an aunt invited, leading Jo into the kitchen.

"Don't mind the dog," she said, as a wet nose pressed against Jo's hand and a warm coat touched her leg.

Jo instinctively scratched the dog's neck right behind his left ear, as he leaned heavily against her. He looked like a petting zoo ewe about to deliver twin lambs. He was a mostly white, medium-sized terrier mix with triangle ears, a pointed nose, wiry fur, and a curled tail.

Spin the Plate

"His name is Goblin," an aunt informed her as she offered the dog a milkbone.

Goblin sniffed at the biscuit disinterestedly, as the other added. "We got him at Halloween."

One aunt scooped Maxwell House into a percolator coffeepot on the stove and set the flame to medium high. In the kitchen, the four sat around a yellow Formica-topped table with a grooved metal ring around the side.

"Francis tells us you're a tattoo artist," one of the aunts chattered excitedly. "He says you're quite talented. It must be wonderful to be artistic and use your talent to bring enjoyment, and joy, and healing, too."

"We just love the show 'Miami Ink,'" she confided. "Does everyone really have a story? You must meet the most interesting people."

It was clear where Francis had acquired his gift of gab, Jo thought.

Jo's eyes wandered through the series of school pictures of a small brown-haired boy hung across the wall of the tiny kitchen. By his teens he was unmistakably Francis. Then Jo settled her gaze on a Lincoln Log cabin showcased on a rounded, built-in, corner shelf with a faded blue ribbon hanging down one side.

An aunt, noticing Jo's gaze, boasted proudly. "Francis did the whole thing himself, every bit of it, you know."

Francis chided. "Come on Auntie, Jo is going to think I peaked at eight."

"Now, Francis," said his aunt patting his arm.

"There is no reason to be modest."

She launched into the story as if it happened yesterday.

"Each child could pick a certain number of pieces and had to decide which to use and make up their own design. When the parents arrived for the presentation, all four sides of the gymnasium displayed the cabins of the lower elementary students. And in the center, right up on the stage–I recognized it right away–right up on the stage was Francis' log cabin," she announced smiling broadly.

"And a bright blue first prize ribbon." Her eyes were wet as she patted Francis' arm again.

With the pot bubbling, filling the kitchen with the rich smell of coffee, one aunt poured three cups of the dark liquid and placed the mugs on the table along with a half gallon carton of cream, a large bowl filled with sugar, and spoons.

The other aunt busied herself catering to Francis, laying out before him a paper plate and knife, a box of Townhouse crackers, a jar of peanut butter, a glass of chocolate milk, and finally a red Macintosh apple expertly prepared on the spot using a circular metal contraption that surrounded the fruit, cored it, and produced six even slices with one press.

She then began emptying the contents from the refrigerator, which Jo noticed where layered on top of one another, onto the table before them. Cold cuts, sliced cheeses, olives, cold cheese ravioli, antipasto, cooked lobster still in the shell, scali bread, butter, biscotti and assorted hard cookies, and ricotta cheese cake.

Spin the Plate

Jo surveyed the feast and noticed Goblin's mild interest as an aunt hand fed him a slice of roast beef. She surmised that Francis' food jag had likely spared him from suffering a similar fate as the bursting-at-the-seams terrier. Jo consumed a respectable portion of the offering, though it seemed to Francis that she was motivated more by politeness than appetite.

As they departed out the front door, there was another round of hugs and an invitation to come back and visit very soon. Jo inhaled deeply a last breath of the warmth and smells of this place. She said goodbye to the aunts and left with Francis to meet her parents.

When they arrived at Jo's family bash, an elderly aunt walked towards them. As she passed beside Jo, she gave her hand a quick squeeze saying almost inaudibly. "So pleased you've come, Juliana." and continued moving forward.

Jo headed across the room and hunkered down in a folding chair in the far corner. Francis pulled up a chair beside her. His repeated attempts to make conversation with Jo failed. Jo scanned the room intently, looking distant as always, but with a furrow deepening in her brow.

Finally Francis asked her. "Mind if I work the crowd?"

"Sure, fine," she murmured.

As he stood, a man strode towards them with a

woman in tow. The man had a heavy build, an ashen face, and a protruding stomach. The woman was trim with a neat salon haircut, color, and curls, wearing a straight black dress and crisp white half jacket. Her lips were pressed in a red line and her arms were crossed tightly at her waist. Francis thought that she must have been beautiful, once.

The man glared at Francis through squinted eyes and said to him. "Juliana didn't tell us she'd be bringing anyone."

Jo turned her eyes to the woman and said. "Hi Ma. This is my friend, Francis."

"Oh, ho! A friend," her father retorted, clamping Francis roughly on the shoulder. "Maybe, a *boy...* friend."

"Come. We need to get acquainted," the large man said, leading the way to the buffet table, where, after Francis piled a plate with Townhouse crackers, her father leaned over to him and whispered at length. Jo could see Francis' jaw was clenched; his posture rigid, awkward. He listened politely, but it was clear to Jo that he wasn't about to get friendly or chatty with her father.

In her husband's absence, Jo's mother became more animated. "Oh, Juliana. Just look at you."

"Why do you insist on wearing that getup," she sniffed. "You look like a farmer."

"For God's sake, they had this *catered*. I still have a closetful of beautiful dresses in your bedroom at home," she went on. "Of course none of those would fit you now..."

Jo interrupted the diatribe in midstream. "You look

well Mother."

She continued deliberately. "No visible bruises. Did he keep it to the rib cage, with the big bash coming up on the horizon?"

Her mother hissed back. "Why do you have to be so hateful."

The woman whirled away. Letting out a soft yelp, she clutched her midsection more tightly.

Jo leaned forward in her chair and pleaded with the retreating back. "Oh Ma, I'm sorry!"

Jo's mother wandered in search of a glass of white wine and her husband.

Jo whispered. "I didn't know."

She chewed the inside of her left thumbnail, and small vertical dents appeared to each side of her forehead.

Afterwards, in the car, Francis' face was drawn and for once his boundless energy drained.

"Wow," he said.

They drove without speaking for a while.

"That's not okay," Francis commented.

CHAPTER 5: Crusades

After the family party, alone at home, Jo felt restless and agitated. Her mind raced. She let the dogs out to pee and gave the rats a treat, but was immune to any other pleas for further attention. She set out, alone. Tonight she would be a vigilante and pose as a member of Pet Ink, a group of tattooed tough guys who had a soft spot for lost, stolen, or mistreated pets and dogs living on the street. Jo was not a joiner, instead she simply claimed an affiliation.

She reached into her side pocket for a list of contact information she'd collected over the past few weeks from lost dog ads and posters. It was amazing how trusting people were who were distraught over a missing canine family member and the amount they would disclose. After an initial interview with the owner, she'd gather information from neighbors, people out on the street, the homeless, or even cops. No one yet questioned her credentials.

On rare occasions she found and delivered the actual dog to the doorstop of his home on a late night ring-and-run. She always claimed, in a note, that the continued success of Pet Ink depended on their members' anonymity. The best reward was a donation to a no kill shelter and for the owners to keep their mouths shut. Other times, by following leads on a stolen pet, she found some other neglected or abused creature even more in need of redemption.

When the mission involved beating up the perpetrator, as it usually did, it made the night crusade all the better. Jo wouldn't mind another stint in prison, if unavoidable. She had arrangements set with a shelter worker for her animals' care, if that should happen, with the phone number memorized for her call from a jail cell. However, whether the abusers had rap sheets or just knew they had it coming, she didn't know. But no one ever reported an incident, yet.

Angrily, list in hand, Jo headed out for the streets.

The next morning as the sun rose over the city, Francis leafed through the work clothes in his closet. He couldn't walk out front in a suit; it would draw too much attention. No matter, because today was casual. It was fine to get dressed in work jeans or slacks at home, which he much preferred over maneuvering into a suit in the men's room at the airport–or in a pinch on the plane. He put his hand on one of the pairs of custom jeans and smiled thinking of the multiple fittings and $1500 price tag. They were his favorite pants, but he wasn't sure of the dress code on the golf course where he would be working today. So, he settled on a pair of pressed khakis. He slipped on soft leather Rockport boat shoes and a light blue polo shirt.

Francis gazed into the tall, thin almost full-length mirror nailed to the wall and was satisfied with the effect. He would blend in just like The Invisible Man everyone plainly saw and no one noticed in an obscure G.K. Chesterton short story murder mystery by that name that he'd read in high school. As an afterthought he put on his own worn jacket for warmth and to blend in with his East Boston neighbors. He could leave the jacket in the car. He also brought a new windbreaker, carefully rolled so it wouldn't wrinkle, to change into later. Then he exited his room out the back door of the house, walked around to the front steps, and waited.

The sun had not fully risen in the sky. He watched the cars drive by, carrying morning-people heading for early jobs, and saw high school kids starting to congregate for the bus. He wished he could tell Jo where he was going, what he was doing, and who he'd be seeing today. Though truthfully, it would not be a particularly interesting day for him. He just wanted to impress her with a little name dropping.

Francis had taken over his parents' business 11 years ago on his 21st birthday. Back then each day was a novel and exciting immersion into the world of wealth, power, beautiful people, politicians, world leaders, the rich, and the famous. As time went on, Francis found it took more power, more wealth, more fame to get that same rush and eventually to have any effect at all.

Francis made an unfortunate discovery long ago: most people will become numb and desensitized by anything, no matter how amazing or disgusting it is at first, simply by doing it over and over, day in and day out. He was increasingly tired of all of it. He pondered whether he was at the same place, mentally, as a veteran septic tank pumper who had been completely grossed out on his first day of work. Francis went on to imagine a young guy just starting out in the profession struggling to hold back from retching, and then, fast forward, the same guy aged a decade barely noticing the stench of human waste surrounding him. Perhaps he, like Francis, felt trapped, but resigned to his lot in life and was just trying to get through the day, with the best part of it being able to spend a few hours outside in the sunshine.

A black Toyota Avalon pulled up to the curb in front of Francis' home. No one in the East Boston neighborhood suspected that veiled behind the tinted windows was a well-known philanthropist and one of the countries richest men. Charles Davis preferred the Porsche. But he knew as long as Francis insisted on living in this dump, it was best to keep a low profile when picking him up. Francis arose from sitting on the front step and quickly jumped into the back seat beside him.

As the driver pulled away from the curb and Francis strapped on his seat belt Charles questioned him. "Are we are we going commercial?"

Francis replied. "No, the private jet. I need to brief you on the way. Beside you tee-off at one."

Francis continued. "We'll come home tonight on Delta though. The red eye."

Charles raised an eyebrow.

"It can't be helped. The Carters are here in town at the Kennedy Library to attend that event with Caroline, and you'll be having breakfast with them in the morning. Hey, at least *you'll* be flying home first class."

"Speaking of class," Charles said with disdain. "I hope you're planning to leave that jacket in the car. God Francis, have you been shopping at the Good Will again?"

Francis waved his L.L. Bean windbreaker in the air. "I've got my work jacket."

Rather then letting it go, Charles pressed. "Let me buy you a coat, for yourself."

"I'm good," Francis replied trying not to sound irritated.

Sometimes Charles got too caught up in the illusion. He almost seemed to forget he was a front man and that he was only playing the role of a billionaire.

Charles Davis, who's birth name was Stuart Clay, had been hired by Francis' father when he was just 15. In high school, Charles was a strong athlete, a promising thespian starring in every annual school play since middle school, popular with classmates, and well-liked by the teachers in his small, rural high school. Francis' father had groomed Charles for the job of the front man, which Francis secretly thought of as "puppet," until Charles' first public appearance at 21.

Since his emergence into the public eye, Charles lived on an allowance, albeit a hefty one. Everything from his penthouse apartments in seven cities within four countries to his Fendi sunglasses and Burluti shoes were on loan to him as payment–or more accurately a bribe–to maintain his role as the man in the public's radar scope. A generous monthly pension fund would insure his silence in his retirement and an inheritance to his children would keep him quiet to his grave. Once a person was accustom to living rich, it was almost impossible for him to go back.

It was freedom from the dependence on living well that was the main reason Francis' parents had lived a modest life. Another reason for their humble lifestyle was that preserving their privacy was more valuable to them than wealth. Finally, his father's job, which Francis had now assumed, demanded a fairly high level of anonymity.

Like his father before him Francis was the middle man; he was the conduit. Francis needed to stay as private and as invisible as possible. He was like the magician's assistant who performed the real magic while Charles, as the magician, took the spotlight mesmerizing the crowd with his smile and his flare. Francis inherited the traits of a good conduit from his father: highly intellectual and non egotistical with a photographic memory. In addition, both father and son had the same strong sense of responsibility and a burning desire to better the world.

The third layer and final player was the sponsor, whom Francis always thought of as the "puppet master," since he pulled the strings. He was the decision maker. The sponsor's identity was a mystery to the front man, a fact that over the years increasingly irritated Charles.

It marveled Francis that Charles had not yet discovered the obvious truth about the sponsor. But as his father liked to say, "Once someone gets into his head that an answer is complex, he loses the ability completely and forever to see the simple solution that is right in front of his face."

Charles and Francis boarded the private jet. There were three pairs of comfortable tan leather seats along either side. A wide space in-between fit a rounded-edge, rectangular conference table anchored to the floor along with the six chairs surrounding it. There was a fully-stocked bar across the back side of the plane.

Francis was trained and certified as an airline steward which afforded a double benefit. Francis was able to listen unobtrusively to meetings between Charles and influential donors or beneficiaries to keep the sponsor informed. And, for trips such as today's, he and Charles could travel alone with just the pilot and meet Federal Aviation Administration regulation for having a steward or stewardess on board a jet with a filed flight plan.

It took Francis about 20 minutes to brief Charles on the essence of the day's upcoming meeting.

"Ted and Jane invited you for golf under the guise of a purely social meeting," Francis began.

"Are they on again?" Charles interrupted.

"Still claiming to be just good friends. Our sources say they've been getting more and more involved in collaborating on something they are calling the Turner Environmental Decade. It's likely they're going to ask for matching funding, which is fine. There certainly are the resources on our end, but they're going to have to ante a good chunk of change on this one upfront. Also, you know how Jane tends to jump from one pet project to the next, so I'm sure the sponsor is going to want payments tied to clear milestones. Just get them talking about the specifics for me, will you, you know the usual stuff, 'That's interesting, tell me more about that.' I'll give you the signal if I need details. It has to be clear that this is seed money. And find out what the global implications are."

Francis could see Charles starting to shift in his seat and eying the bar, even though it was barely 8:00 in the morning.

"Just one more thing," Francis went on. "I'll need to call the sponsor to get the final okay. When I have all I need, I'll say something like 'Hey Boss, you want me to make that call to New York?'"

At this Charles perked up. "So he's in New York. Living in New York?"

Francis sighed. "I don't know where he lives."

And, continued to lie, "or any idea who he is. He's *1 on my cell, that's how I contact him. That's all I know. If he needs anything he gets the message to me."

Francis reclined in the leather seat, feigning exhaustion, and closed his eyes. Charles was an exceptional front man, but he tired Francis. For the person with whom Francis spent most of his waking hours, the two had surprisingly little in common.

"Hey, Francis," Charles began.

"Hmmm," he replied.

"Are you coming tomorrow?" Charles asked.

Francis wished he could. He didn't know how much longer Jimmy and Rosalynn would continue to make public appearances.

"No," Francis said. "Philip will cover the Carters."

Francis hoped Charles wasn't getting chatty on him. If the faked exhaustion failed he would pull the New Testament out of his back pocket and try to engage Charles in some theology. Francis wondered briefly if using scriptures to be left alone was a sin? Probably.

Suddenly, a wave of sincere tiredness hit Francis, and he relaxed into the leather. He thought about Jimmy and Rosalynn Carter. Jimmy had turned 85 and just welcomed the birth of his latest great grandchild into the world. Francis first met the couple years ago; Jimmy was one of those rare people who would strike a conversation with anyone from any walk of life. Francis at the time was posing as Charles' handyman. Jimmy had questions about installing affordable electric wiring and wondered whether Francis might have some time to help with a new housing development in New Orleans. Francis found it hard to resist his advances, despite knowing full well that even causal conversation could jeopardize being invisible and his success as the conduit.

So it would be Francis' backup, Philip, who would cover the Carters. Philip, whose name was really James, had apprenticed under Francis for the past year as his stand-in in the role of the middle man. He was much better than Francis was in deflecting friendly overtures. It was just one of the many ways the student had surpassed the teacher.

"Philip" as he called himself, was always thinking. He had an unusual ability to shift easily between the big picture and minute detail as called for by the situation. His name change was one example. "Jesus,

Francis, I can't go with 'James.' It's too obvious. I sound like a goddamn butler."

Hours later, Francis was awakened by a slightly bumpy landing at a private airfield about 30 miles northeast of Rancho Palos Verdes, an affluent Los Angeles suburb built on the bluffs overlooking the Pacific Ocean. Their limousine driver met them at the jet. Awaiting them in the wrap around back seat area was a hot plate of Mahi Mahi and dirty rice with fresh pineapple for Charles and "the usual" for Francis. They ate on the drive and arrived at Trump National Golf Club shortly before 1:00 pm local time.

Francis had met, or more accurately been in the company of, Ted Turner and Jane Fonda a half dozen times over the years. A broad smile and hint of a Spanish accent produced the desired comfortably disinterested response. It was a hot but not scorching day in Southern California. The sun felt good on Francis' skin like going back a season to an end-of-June Boston summer day.

The business side of the game was quickly initiated and presented mostly by Jane with Ted filling in details and numbers. At the eleventh hole, Jane, Ted, and Charles had diverted their attention whole-heartedly to the golf game. Francis gave Ted's golf ball a quick rub on his cloth and rested it on the tee. At least caddying gave Francis something to do. In his mind, the only thing more dull than golfing was watching other people golf.

Francis surreptitiously glanced at his watch for the fifth time in the past seven minutes. Thank God, it was just before 3:00 pm. Time to make the call. Francis excused himself and searched for a private spot, well out of earshot of Charles. He settled on one side of the hexagonal bench in a deserted gazebo a short distance from the clubhouse. Francis was surprised at the feel of perspiration on his palms. He wiped his hands on one of the still clean golf ball cloths in his back pocket, pulled out his cell phone, and dialed *1.

Jo picked up on the third ring.

"Hey," she said. She sounded surprised, but not disappointed, to hear his voice. "I just went on break."

"I know," said Francis. "It's six o'clock. Let me guess. You're in the so called break room enjoying the silence after clicking off the credits to Oprah, relaxing on the black faux leather chair, opening a Tupperware of lasagna, and unwrapping your provolone and salami on scali bread."

Jo put her salami sandwich down with half the cellophane still in place.

"Creeper," she thought, her eyes darting along the walls and ceiling of the room.

"Do you have a camera feed?" she blurted out accusingly, as she examined the base of a table lamp with suspicion.

"Sorry," Francis apologized. "Conversations stick with me. You told me when you have a dinner break, and I saw the party leftovers your cousin packed for you."

Silence.

"Stupid, stupid, stupid," Francis thought. He prayed, "Don't let me blow it now." and barreled ahead.

"So anyways, I was thinking we could meet Sunday at 11:00 at that café we passed on the way to the diner. You know, the one with the green awning. I think it's called Teedo's." Francis knew it was Teedo's Outdoors Café. He also remembered dozens of descriptive features about the place, but was careful this time to avoid saying too much.

Francis paused.

Nothing.

He continued. "I've been thinking about what you told me in the car. A lot. I had an idea."

Despite herself, Jo was intrigued.

"This idea, how about I float it by you on Sunday?" Francis suggested.

"Uh...Okay. Sure."

"Good," Francis replied and quickly changed the subject.

"So what's new. Beat anyone up lately?" he joked.

"Yah, I came across a guy last night who was thinking about stringing up a decrepit old tom cat to a barbed wire fence. Let's just say I dissuaded him from that thought," Jo replied.

"How about you?" Jo asked. "Earning a living? Did you remember the tin can today? Any good tips?"

Francis smiled and feigned insult. "Most of my spendable income comes from cashing in deposit bottle empties, if you must know."

"But no, today I've been busy finishing a political

thriller. What do you think about the idea that all charismatic leaders including several presidents from Roosevelt to Reagan are hired actors, puppets of brilliant, albeit socially awkward, closet billionaires?" Francis began.

Twenty minutes later Francis said goodbye to Jo. Rushing over the plush gentle slopes, he felt like he was floating above the greens. In five days, not counting today or Sunday, he would see Jo again.

As soon as Francis caught sight of Charles, even from a distance, he knew the man was irritated. Charles could be a baby about having to caddy himself and was embarrassed knowing his companions were not accustomed to self-service golfing either.

"Damn it Francis," Charles said. "We're down two holes."

Francis bristled. He'd have a talk with Charles later.

For now he covered up his feelings with a grin and a loud. "Sorry, Boss."

As Francis approached, Charles handed him two golf balls.

In one sweeping motion Francis leaned in to take the objects and whispered into Charles' ear. "The sponsor is onboard. Let's do this."

CHAPTER 6: The Sentence

The following Sunday at Teedo's café, over Jo's hot coffee with extra cream, extra sugar and Francis' tall, cold glass of chocolate milk, she asked him in a sarcastic tone. "So, how do you like my parents?"

He said. "You know Jo, all of it…it's just not okay."

"Yah, I know," she said.

Then after a few seconds she revealed. "I've stopped by the Newton Police station three times over the years. I've rehearsed the words saying them over and over in front of a mirror, 'I'd like to report a crime.' How hard could it be?"

"Very difficult, I'd imagine," Francis replied.

"Well each time the words got caught in my throat and I asked for directions instead," she said.

"The last time when I was there waiting, a woman actually reported a rape. It was…ah, educational."

Francis asked. "So what happened? How does it work?"

Jo explained. "The officer at the front desk was a woman–named Officer Murray–otherwise, I would have walked out right then. She had that no-nonsense cop look. Hair pulled back and uniform complete with the gun, billy club, pepper spray, and a not-exactly-slimming bullet proof vest. Anyways," Jo continued. "She had a nice voice, kind of soothing and asked the woman 'What happened hon?' The woman came right out with it 'I've been raped.'"

"Things moved quickly after that," Jo remembered. The cop hit a button near her shoulder that activated a microphone and said, "Dispatch, we have a 261." Within a few seconds an athletic man joined them from a behind a locked door just a few feet away. He introduced himself to the woman as Sergeant Lucier and then with a nodded to the cop at the desk said, "I'll cover this, Cindy."

"As soon as I saw it was a man who would hear the details I almost bolted, but I was curious about what would happen next."

Francis said. "So, what happened?"

Jo continued. "They moved across the room. I followed as far as the water cooler and poured myself a cup so I could still hear them, but just barely. He asked her her name and whether she was injured. It turns out that she had waited several days since the incident to report it. He called off the ambulance, which was on the way. Then he said to her, 'We're going to go in the back and you're going to tell me everything.'"

Jo concluded. "Then I took off. I spend every waking minute trying to *not* remember these episodes. I can't imagine spilling out all 128 of them to some stranger, the whole time wondering if any of it is giving him a hard on."

Francis said. "You know Jo it might not be like that. Maybe it would be freeing. You wouldn't be judged. It's a conversation that needed to happen long ago."

Jo thought about it for a minute. "I might be able to say some of it to someone. One time. If they were trustworthy. And, I knew there was no record, and they would never repeat what I said. But I don't want to be dragged through the mud, saying it in front of a cop, and then a lawyer, and then in a courtroom while some court reporter types it all down for a permanent record that who knows how many people read."

Francis said. "Well, it doesn't necessarily even have to go to trial."

As they finished their afternoon breakfast at the café, Francis said. "I know someone. He owes me a favor. He's very good."

Jo seemed to be wavering.

Francis said. "I've known him for years and would trust him with my life. I think you'll like him."

Jo acquiesced. "Yeah, okay."

He and Jo took the next train downtown to meet with the lawyer. As they rode, Francis said, "Let me tell you a little bit about Jay. First of all, he's a very good friend, and I know he'll do this. At no cost. Second, when I say he's good, I mean spectacular. You know Alan Dershowitz?"

"Sure. I've seen 'Reversal of Fortune.'" Plus, Jo recalled the summer she suffered through Keisha's obsession with the Court TV televised O.J. Simpson trial re-run which played in the shop's break room for an excruciating 134 days straight.

"Jay went to Harvard Law and was one of Alan's top students," Francis told her. "Jay started out as a defense attorney, but quickly found he was much more sympathetic towards the victims. So, now he's a prosecutor, and a good one. Anyway, he's the one who handles these cases and is certain to get it."

"Yeah. Well, I've never heard of him."

"That's because whereas Dershowitz is a master of the high profile cases, Jay only goes low profile. Jay's specialty is not going to trial. And, getting the injured party what they want or need. Since he wins nearly every case that goes to trial, most defendants plead-out to make a deal. Basically, his intellect and intuition are so far beyond any competitor's that he's able to set up the game so that he can only win. Going against him is like playing chess with Karpov."

Jo knew better than to ask, "Who's Karpov?" She wanted Francis to keep on topic; there would be time another day to hear about the history of chess masters.

"By the way, you'll see in Jay's office that he has a glass chess game. He loves playing; usually I'll go a few games. I *was* president of the chess club at East Boston High."

Jo remained expressionless.

"I can tell you're impressed," Francis interjected. "Anyway, my point is that I'm pretty good. My record so far with Jay is getting to play eight moves before he gets checkmate. With Jay, in chess or the courtroom, it's not a question of who will win, only how long it will take."

"Jay's other hobbies are poker and magic. He claims the lessons should be tax deductible as a business expense. He says these skills come into play as much as any of his Harvard Law School courses."

When they arrived, Jay Yarmo was waiting in his

office. He seemed to be expecting them. Jay was a bear of a man with clear blue eyes that reminded Jo of a husky. He had salt and pepper hair that had started to gray at 20 and then froze half way through. Now in his 50s, there was still almost as much pepper as salt. He spoke slowly and emanated calm. He asked Jo for a quick summary, thankfully not requiring many details. He rapidly assimilated the data and asked a few follow-up questions, such as her father's age and medical history. He let Jo know when he had heard all he needed.

Jay cut right to the chase. "What are you looking for? How long? Best case."

Jo immediately responded. "128 years."

Jay clarified. "So, he'd get out when he's 200?"

Jay let Jo consider that. It was important that she be practical; vindictiveness only bogged down the proceedings.

After a pause Jay resumed. "Okay, let me explain. Your father committed several crimes. A repeated one is called Aggravated Felonious Sexual Assault, which is touching a minor child inappropriately. Can I ask you, did the abuse happen solely within the state of Massachusetts?"

Jo wondered why that mattered and answered warily. "No. Also in our summer rental, in Maine."

Jay asked. "When did you first remember about the abuse?"

Jo answered immediately. "I've never forgotten any of it."

Jay thought for a second. "The problem we run into is the statute of limitations. In Massachusetts, it's just three years from the time of occurrence, from the age of 18, or in the case of repressed memories, three years from when the victim remembers the abuse for the first time."

Jo glared at him incredulously. She fumed in disbelief.

"What are you telling me?"

Then, without giving Jay any time to answer, Jo squeezed her hand into a tight fist and slammed the ball of it into the table like a gavel; her breath came out in short blasts through her nose. This was impossible. The words "statute of limitations" and "three years" hammered through her brain. Everything he'd done to her, all of it was null and void by the passage of a few years time. How stupid she was to think the legal system, so notably absent in the past, would protect her now. Apparently they were in on it too.

"I need to take a walk," she said stumbling out of her chair.

Jay took hold of both Jo's hands encapsulating them in his strong steady ones and pressed them onto the table. His clear blue eyes anchored her in place. Jay spoke softly and with conviction.

"Don't worry about it. We'll get him," he promised her.

Jo suddenly felt lightheaded and collapsed back into her seat.

Jay said. "Listen to me Jo. We may not be able to bring criminal charges in Massachusetts, but Maine has no statute of limitations. We can bring a criminal case there. We can bring a civil case in Massachusetts, at a minimum."

Spin the Plate

Jo calmed a bit. "Okay," she thought. "Maine's not that far away. We could go to court there."

Jay, as though reading her thoughts, explained. "We can do the deposition right here in Boston. And, Jo, it won't go to trial. Another thing, Maine has an agreement with Massachusetts for convicted residents to serve in Massachusetts, and the state will pay the costs. Think about how far you want to distance yourself from him. Being allowed to serve in-state is a good bargaining chip for me to bring to the table."

Jay proposed. "What about this? How about 15 years most likely at the Western Mass Correctional Facility with 30 years suspended. That means even a minor transgression after the 15 and he's locked up for 30 more. While in prison he'll have to complete a sexual offender counseling course. And he won't be allowed any unsupervised visits with minors for 45 years."

Jo hesitated.

Jay persisted. "I'll need your help, but it will be in the form of a deposition. Just me, you, your father, and his lawyer. He may want your mother there, and you can have a family member or Francis present. No jury, no trial. I'll prep you with all you need to say and do. We'll hand pick a few snippets of attacks that were perpetrated, but only enough to bait his lawyer."

Still Jo hesitated.

Jay finished. "It won't go to trial. And, at his age and health he'll most likely come out in a box."

Somehow Jo, who trusted no one, felt safe in this man's hands.

"Fine," Jo said.

It was then she shared her secret for the first time. "You know I have tapes. Of him. Of the crime."

"I'm not willing to let anyone, not even me or you, see them," Jo clarified. "I'm only telling you in case it helps you to know about them."

Jay was thrilled at the news, but didn't let on. He had the same giddy feeling he always got the moment the path to a checkmate laid itself out in front of him.

He asked in a serious tone. "Does your father know that you have the tapes?"

"Yes," Jo said.

"Very good. That's all we need. I don't need to watch them. Just tell me about these recordings. Tell me everything."

"A few years back," Jo began, "I was minding the house for my parents who were away for a long weekend of leaf peeking in Connecticut. I came by each day to check on the cat and bring in the mail and newspaper. The thermostat was turned down to 65, and even though it was too warm to wear my jacket inside, I was cold without it. So, I went into my father's bedroom to borrow a sweater."

She paused.

Jay said. "Take your time."

She took in a long breath. After several seconds she went on. "There in his dresser drawer, beneath the sweaters, I found two VCR tapes labeled 'Home Movies,' not dated, but with a small red 'x' in the lower right-hand corner. I thought it was strange. When I was growing up, my parents did have a movie camera. But, vacations and holidays were marked by increased drinking and a lot of yelling so mostly the camera stayed forgotten in its carry case or set up, but turned off, in a tripod in one corner."

"I pushed one of the movies into the VCR player. What I saw got me so dizzy I was sure I was going to throw up. It was me on the TV, five years old, wearing my Easter dress. I knew after just a few seconds that episode 26 was about to play. Not in my memory either. The real thing."

Jo remembered struggling for a moment to stay standing and gulping back warm saliva filling her mouth, preparing her to vomit.

"I pressed 'Stop.'"

She clearly recalled her one and only thought. "To this day, that sick bastard is using me to jack off."

The realization set her heart pumping, filling her veins with blood and a rush of energy.

She said angrily. "So, I ransacked the house going from attic to basement, emptying every box, dumping each drawer, searching any VCR tape sized space."

"I pretty much destroyed the place," Jo said with some satisfaction. "In all I found a total of six of those tapes."

All six were identically labeled, "Home Movies" with a red "x." These she put aside. The rest of the VCR tapes, commercial or home-made, she smashed. The six movies she wrapped in three layers of grocery store plastic bags to transport them home. The next day she bought a fireproof strong box and stored the movies under the floorboards in her living room. Perhaps she had always known she'd need them later.

Jay queried. "Did your parents confront you? Did your father ever try to recover the tapes?"

Jo replied. "No. Not surprisingly, like everything else, the whole incident was swept under the rug. My parents never even mentioned that the house was trashed. And my father never said a thing about the missing tapes."

Jay asked her. "Do you have any G-rated tapes of the same brand?"

Jo answered. "No. I don't have any normal home movies."

Jay said. "That's okay, all you need to do is buy one of a similar type and paste the label onto it. No writings or markings are necessary. Make sure you leave the other tapes at home and bring just the blank one to the deposition."

He told Jo he would let the defense attorney bait her. Her job was to feign building anger until Jay gave the signal. At that moment Jo would blurt out a line about having something to show them. Jay confided in her it would cause quite a dramatic Perry Mason moment as she, at the same time, produced the tape from her overall bib.

"Trust me," Jay assured her. "It takes only the slightest provocation to get the guilty to think they see what they are hiding. And dreading."

After the initial meeting with Jay, the legal proceedings moved rapidly. Everything unfolded just as Jay had predicted, almost as though he'd written the script for a

Spin the Plate

one act play.

At 10:00 am Monday Jay called Jo. "We have an indictment. The police just picked up your father and he's on his way in. Twenty-one counts of sexual battery on a child, including rape of a child. Each one carries a sentence of up to 30 years."

At 4:00 pm, Jay called Jo back. "Your father hired a former colleague of mine, Barbara Anderson, to represent him. She was well-trained in my old job as a district attorney and now she's a high-priced defense lawyer. She's very good."

"Will he still go to jail?" Jo inquired.

"I'll do all I can to make sure that happens," Jay assured her.

He explained. "Barbara wants a quick date, which your father is entitled to under the sixth amendment."

"How quick?" Jo wondered aloud.

"We'll have a deposition later in the week. She wants us to be as unprepared as possible. It will be right here in the courthouse, in one of the conference rooms upstairs."

At the deposition that Thursday, there were five of them positioned around a heavy pine table. On one side was Barbara and Jo's father. Across from her father sat Francis. His eyes were closed, and he seemed to be humming or maybe singing to himself under his breath. He looked peaceful as though he might be about to smile. Next to him, and across from Barbara, sat Jay. Jo was seated to Jay's right and as far diagonally across the table as possible from her father. Jo's mother was not present.

"No big surprise there," Jo thought.

Barbara dove directly into the proceedings. "You know Ms. Orsiano, you are alleging an extremely serious charge, namely the rape of a child. When we go to trial, prosecution must show beyond a reasonable doubt, that the defendant, your dad here, had unlawful penetration of the alleged victim or the victim had unlawful penetration of the defendant, the alleged victim was less than 13 years old, and the defendant acted intentionally, knowingly, or recklessly.

Barbara continued. "When we go to trial this is how it will go."

Jo felt a hint of panic at the repeated phrase "*when we go to trial.*"

Jo glanced at Jay and relaxed some at the barely perceptible shake of his head.

Barbara informed her. "The jury will hear my opening statement, where I will say something to the effect of: 'My client, Bill Orsiano, is innocent. The testimony you will hear will be shocking, saddening, graphic, grotesque, and you will be angry when you hear it and you will want to find a villain. But the villain isn't Bill. You will get to know Bill, as I have, and hearing his story you will know, as I know, that he is a loving father who would never hurt his or any child."

"You're going to hear testimony about 128 alleged 'episodes' from Bill's daughter, Juliana," said Barbara skeptically, using her fingers to make quote marks in the air. "She'll tell you about so called episode 22 when a vibrator was placed on her private area and episode 81 when her anus was penetrated. And she will be certain she is telling the truth. Listen carefully to her testimony. It is in the details that you will find reasonable doubt. You will also hear testimony about a concept called suggestibility. Suggestibility is when there are false memories in someone's brain. Juliana will not perjure herself when she says she remembers certain events. But the events *never happened*. Or they didn't happen the way she said they did. But it doesn't matter what I say. The only thing that matters is the testimony of the experts. Expert testimony will prove to you that the memories that Juliana says are real are, in fact, not real. When you listen to the testimony, you will conclude that no one knows that happened 20 or more years ago. And if you do, you must return a verdict of not-guilty."

Jo wanted to punch her. She realized her right hand which was resting on her right thigh had curled into a tight fist. Relaxing her fingers and stretching them out straight, she drew both hands from hiding and placed them palm down on the table in front of her.

"This is how it will go next," Barbara pushed forward relentlessly. "I will start by calling Juliana Orsiano to the stand."

"The bailiff will come to you with a Bible and customary 'Do you swear the testimony you give will be the truth, the whole truth, and nothing but the truth, so help you God?'"

"Then Ms. Orsiano, you must say what you know

happened, not just what you think happened or may have imagined happened. But what really happened."

Barbara paused, met Jo's eyes, and said softly. "For God's sake do you know what you are putting your father through?"

Barbara Anderson waited long enough for the accusation to settle.

Then resuming her lawyer tone, Barbara said. "We'll start with the demographics. Age, where you live, what you do for a living, where you work, how old you are, and your relationship to the defendant. We'll move next into your relationship with your father today: house sitting and other favors you perform, family gatherings you attend, that sort of thing. We'll discuss other intimate relationships that you maintain today, such as any long-term close friendships you may have. Next, we'll get to how often you have these memories or thoughts about your father and why you suddenly decided to bring them up now. When we get beyond all that, you'll have to recall all 128 of the alleged episodes."

"Let's you and I go through a little bit of testimony Ms. Orsiano, just to see what it is like. Think carefully about whether you want to do this. Whether you are really able to do this."

Jo stole a sideways glance in Jay's direction. His nod let her know everything was as planned and to just go with it. Beyond him she could see Francis with his eyes closed, body in a slight rhythmic rocking. He looked calm. Jo was careful not to look in the direction of her father; she imagined she could feel the heat of his anger simmering and rising.

Spin the Plate

Barbara shuffled her notes in preparation. Jo swallowed hard as Barbara pressed down the Record button on the tape recorder in the middle of the table. Jo was sworn in and had to forcibly will herself to stay seated.

Barbara began the questioning. "Tell me what happened on what you call episode 26."

Jo answered immediately. "Episode 26 happened the day before Easter when I was five. My father raped me in my bedroom. I asked him to stop and he didn't."

"Jo, could you take a look at this?" Barbara handed her a piece of paper. "Could you tell me what it is?"

"It's a receipt from a hotel."

"Could you tell me the date."

"April 7th, 1985."

"Could you tell me where the hotel is?"

"Miami, Florida."

"And could you tell me who was staying in the hotel."

"Bill and Michaela Orsiano."

"Is that the defendant?"

"Yes. And my mother."

"I'd like this marked exhibit A. Now, Ms. Orsiano, please take this. It is a 1985 calendar. How old were you in 1985?"

A pause. "Let me think…uh…Five," Jo said.

"Please turn to April. What date is Easter Sunday."

"April 8th."

"So if you father was in Florida with your mom, how could he have been in Belmont raping you on that very day?"

Jo felt the panic return and intensify, even though she recognized this was the exact scenario Jay had predicted.

"I'm not lying. I was wearing my Easter Dress. He raped me. I know he did."

"In your bedroom. When he was in Florida."

"It happened so long ago; maybe I was wearing the dress for professional pictures. We have a picture of me in that dress in the hallway. I can't remember details. I know he raped me."

"That was a long time ago," Barbara said sympathetically. "I know it's hard to remember what really happened."

Jo wished she could jump up and smack her. She was being painted as a liar. She knew she was telling the truth. She remembered all the details that mattered.

"I'm not lying."

Jo caught Jay out of the corner of her eye, drumming his fingers on the table. Thank God, the signal.

Picking her words carefully, Jo announced. "I have something I want you to see."

From the inside of her bib Jo pulled out a VCR tape.

"What is that a video of?" Barbara demanded.

Barbara turned first to Jay and then to Bill flushing slightly. "I was never told about any tapes."

Then she exploded. "Come on Jay. You know full well you can't spring evidence on me. You know 'disclosure.' Plan on spending tomorrow in court."

Jay feigned innocence. With Barbara berating him, Jay was oblivious to what was ensuing on the far left side corner of the table. For the first time in the proceedings Jo peeked in the direction of her father. What she saw made her stare, unable to look away. His face was red and turning purple with the veins in his neck bulging. Everyone around Jo and her father began to disappear into a fog. Jo was transported back in time with her father's words.

"You little shit. You wouldn't dare."

Suddenly, it was just her and him. Bill stood up so rapidly that his chair fell backwards. He grabbed the corner of the heavy pine table. Francis' eyes flew open. He, Jay, and Barbara were stunned into inaction. Jo, in a combination of knowing her father and the well-practiced Sumo moves, quickly leapt away from the table and stood ready to act.

Her father took hold of the table with both hands and overturned it. The VCR tape cracked under the heavy weight. Barbara was thrown back, and Jay and Francis were barricaded on the other side of the overturned table.

"Goddamn that man is strong," was all Jo could think.

Jo squared off, arms at her sides moving into a wide-legged stance with both hands curling into fists. Suddenly the obvious was clear. This was it, the true purpose of years of intensive training. He was standing in front of her, furious, eyes burning, aiming to punish her. She instinctively lowered her eyes, from habit, and then purposefully kept her gaze downward to draw him in. In her vertical peripheral vision she could see him advancing. An indescribable euphoria filled her. The position of the table and the shock of the unfolding events kept Jay and Francis from coming to Jo's defense. Barbara crawled toward their side of the table and covered her head with her briefcase.

"Good," Jo didn't want to hurt them in the fray.

Her father stomped toward Jo like a crazed bull. Five more steps and her fist would smash into his face crumpling him like a straw man. She knew once she started to beat him she would be unable to stop until she was forcibly pulled off and restrained or better yet her arms tired of pummeling his still, lifeless body.

At that moment, the door to the deposition room crashed opened and two police officers, faster than linebackers and just as huge, leapt at her father and knocked him face first to the floor. There was a sickening thud as the large man hit the hardwood floor. The sound provided little consolation to Jo for the abrupt ending to her only recently discovered deepest desire. One officer drew his gun as the other pinned Jo's father with a knee in the small of his back as he reached for handcuffs and then forcibly shackled the man's wrists behind him. The officers pulled him to his feet and, after a quick thumbs up signal directed toward the closed circuit camera mounted at ceiling height on the far wall, they roughly shoved him out of the room.

Ninety minutes later the two lawyers met privately.

Barbara started off the negotiations. "We'd like to

offer a deal. Obstruction of justice. Child porn. He knew of the existence of the tapes, but didn't tell authorities. Ten with five suspended."

Jay responded. "Twenty, outside New England, in a level-3 sex offender facility."

Barbara answered. "Okay, I get there are Brady considerations on the rape and battery counts, yes. But not on the filming and transportation across state lines. *If* these tapes are real. And, we're not saying he made them. Just that he knew about them."

Jay asked. "So…bottom line."

Barbara said. "Fifteen years in the Western Mass Correctional Facility."

Jay countered. "Throw in 30 years suspended and no unsupervised visits with children and we've got a deal."

Barbara agreed. "Yes, my client is amenable. Fifteen years with 30 years suspended."

Jay went back and told Jo. "Okay, we've got what you wanted."

Jo said. "And, he's going to admit he's guilty?"

"Sort of. Not to rape of a child or sexual battery. He's admitting to having knowledge of tapes involving sex and a minor."

Jo's heart was racing. She was furious. "So he doesn't have to admit that he raped me? No. Forget it. We'll just go to trial if we have to. He has to admit it or forget it."

Jay cautioned Jo. "We can do whatever you want. If we go that route you've got a taste of what we'll be in for. Barbara is setting up a case of suggestibility. She has some very good experts who are going to testify that the memories you have are false. Her star witness is Elizabeth Hoffman, who has testified in over 1,000 cases. She's very good, Jo. When you go to trial you put your destiny in the hands of the jurors. It's only a slight chance, but without showing the tapes your father might walk."

"And Jo," Jay added. "One more thing to think about. If you don't do this now, he's free on bail until the trial. You'd know better than anyone, do you think he's a flight risk? Would he take off for Belize or something?"

"Did you know Belize is the only country in this hemisphere that doesn't have an extradition treaty with the United States?" Francis interjected, trying to be helpful.

Jo considered her options for a minute and then asked Jay. "If I agree to this, would he spend his first night in prison tonight?"

Jay responded. "I'm sure that could be arranged."

Resigned, Jo said. "Shit. Fine."

From then on it was a blur of activity. There was an intimate meeting in chambers–the five from the deposition in an audience with the judge.

Judge Sweeney sat behind a large mahogany desk, stone-faced and dressed in black robes. The five sat in a slight arc in front of him. Jo and her father were seated on the far edges separated by as many chairs as possible. The police officer who had handcuffed Bill during the altercation earlier that day stood directly behind Jo's left shoulder looking grim and never taking his eyes off her father. In the presence of the judge, Jo's father looked subdued and old.

"Mr. Orsiano. Will you rise sir. I understand you are pleading guilty to obstruction of justice charges."

"Yes, Judge," said Bill stumbling to his feet.

"You understand this means that you are giving up your constitutional rights to a trial by jury and also your protection of self-incrimination. You also understand that you will be sentenced immediately and you will go to the Western Massachusetts House of Correction tonight."

"Yes, Judge."

"Therefore I sentence you to 15 years in the Western Massachusetts House of Correction with 30 years suspended. While in prison, you must complete a sexual offender counseling course and you will not be allowed any unsupervised visits with minors for 45 years."

"Yes, Judge," said Bill quietly, almost meekly.

Before leaving the courthouse Jo asked Jay about any forms she'd need to fill out for prison visitation. Jay examined Jo critically wondering what her motives might be. Her face was emotionless.

Finally he said with some misgiving. "Okay. Once the paperwork is ready, I'll have it overnighted to you."

Three Sundays later, two days after receiving approval papers and instruction by mail, Jo and Francis made the first of their weekly three hour drives to the northwest-most point of the state.

"You know, you don't have to do this Jo," Francis said for the third time.

"I know I don't have to. I need to," was the best that she could explain.

Francis let it go. He'd just as soon let the bastard rot in jail. But he knew Jesus was a big advocate of forgiveness, mercy, visiting prisoners, and honoring one's parents no matter how undeserving. What's more, Francis believed dissuading someone from following His wishes was a most serious sin. *"... whoever causes one of these little ones who believe in me to sin, it would be better for him to have a great millstone fastened around his neck and to be drowned in the depth of the sea."* So he kept his mouth shut.

Jo knew there was no one else to take care of her father. She knew all too well her mother would not step up; it was a lifetime pattern of having her mother's responsibilities fall on her shoulders. As in many Italian families, it was understood from birth that the youngest daughter's role, and beyond that, her very reason for being, was to take care of the father in his old age. And this was even more expected in the case of an only-daughter. Jo would demand justice, but she could not desert him.

They drove the length of Route 2 West in silence. The late Sunday morning traffic was light. A few weeks ago the leaves had been a brilliant array of autumn colors. Now the trees looked haggard in their threadbare red and yellow coats with some of the leaves turning to brown while still clinging to the branches. Jo stared through the windshield and was mesmerized by the whish, whish, whish of the passing trees. She traveled in her mind to a place she rarely went. This was a memory she'd never shared with anyone and one that never forced itself upon her.

She wakes up from a bad dream and climbs out of bed. She glances down the hallway and considers crawling into bed with Mommy. Mommy finished her drinks and light yellow pill hours ago and would be cold and unresponsive. Instead, she turns toward the den which is dark except for the dimming and brightening glow of the television. Daddy is watching a black and white movie, alone, in the dark. She settles into his lap. As sleep overcomes her, he whispers into her hair. 'You're all I have, baby. You know I love you.'"

Jo and Francis finally arrived to the prison grounds on the outskirts of North Adams. They drove up a long, unpaved road to an area marked "Reception and Visitors." Jo parked the car and could see a huge grey complex.

"Wait here," she said to Francis.

"Let me come up with you," he suggested. "I filled out the paperwork, too."

"No," she responded. "I'll be right back."

"No rush," he said.

"This won't take long," Jo informed him.

As Jo approached, she saw bars on the windows and, at the end of one of the wings, a courtyard with a paved area and several basketball hoops. Two fences topped with razor-sharp wire about 20 feet apart surrounded the buildings and the courtyard. There was a third fence about 10 feet high that had an imposing, believable sign that read "Electric Fence. Do Not Touch" with the skull and crossbones symbol.

Jo remembered the rules. Don't bring anything in except for your license and a roll of quarters for the vending machines. She had taken her license out of her wallet which she left in the car, along with the car keys still in the ignition so Francis could listen to the radio, and, of course, left her hand gun, too, which she furtively slipped into the glove compartment.

She went up the stairs and opened the door to reception. There were lockers cemented around the walls and two long metal benches in the middle. At the far side of the wall behind highly frosted, bulletproof glass was the guard; only the featureless silhouette of a person of undetermined gender could be seen within.

"Good morning," a voice said. "Here for visiting hours?"

"Yes," her voice echoed loudly.

"Speak into the microphone."

Jo found a long goose-neck microphone and said into it that she was here to see her father.

"May I have your license please?" the voice said.

Out popped a metal compartment, like the kind at a bank drive-through window. Jo put her license into it and clipped it in place.

"Are you on the visitor's list?"

"Yes," she said. "I filled out the forms weeks ago. The letter said I could see him anytime." About two minutes of silence rang in her ears. She wondered whether she'd made a wasted trip.

"We'll get him," broke the silence.

"This is my first time visiting."

Spin the Plate

"I know. Do you have anything on your person?"

Jo showed the roll of quarters.

"You'll need to unwrap them and put them in the napkin I give you."

Jo followed the instructions. She could tell they were watching.

"Anything else?" the voice commanded.

"No."

"Could you please show the inside of your pockets?"

Jo did.

"And the bib of the overalls."

Jo opened and exposed the back side.

Out popped the bank teller drawer. "Keys, please."

Jo complied, placing house keys she'd forgotten about onto the tray.

"You can pick them up when you leave, along with your license. Step through the security gate, please."

Jo passed through the doorframe style metal detector. There were no beeps. "You're all set. Follow the signs. Exit to the door on the right. Don't forget your quarters. On the table." These Jo had neglected to retrieve after going though the metal detector.

"Oh...okay."

Jo stood at the prison entrance in front of a large, sliding glass door made of thick glass and metal reinforcements all around. There were two video cameras that she could see. She stood there for about 45 seconds, and, suddenly, it opened. She went into a holding compartment about as big as a large elevator. On the opposite side was a second door with a window on it. Another voice told her to stand in the middle.

The door to the reception area closed with a loud shutting noise, and then a pronounced locking mechanism a few seconds later. She was expecting the second door to open immediately. It didn't. She just stared at it.

She didn't have a watch, so after standing and waiting a few seconds she started counting to herself. On the count of 87, that door opened and a kind sounding voice said to follow the signs. A few steps down a long, white corridor with painted white walls and no windows, she heard the door behind her close. And "Thunk" with a sound of finality. Then "Click" and lock: the sound of no escape. She looked back thinking, with some satisfaction, of what it must have been like for her father to hear those noises, what they meant to him.

There were posters on the walls that seemed out of place. Industrial posters like "Bend With Your Knees" with a stick figure-like drawing of a person lifting something. And obscure admonitions like "Please Keep Your Feet Off The Walls."

Jo couldn't help but think. "Are these major problems here?"

When she entered the visitors' room, she saw prisoners talking in low voices to their visiting wives and girlfriends, some with their children playing at the tables. One man sat on the floor with a boy about two years old. Jo also noted there were several guards positioned around the room. One of them asked her name and told her she could sit at whatever table she'd like. There were diner-style square stainless steel tables and short round stainless steel stools. The metal chairs and the tables they surrounded were bolted to the floor. The seat was more comfortable than Jo expected, though cold at first.

There were 20 or so vending machines in a semi-circle around the room encasing ice cream, candy, chips, cookies, frozen dinners, Coke, Pepsi, and water. The tile on the floor was off white, except for around the perimeter where the vending machines were–that area was deep blue.

One of the soft-spoken guards told her she could put her quarters on the table and reminded her that her dad couldn't touch them, but she could buy things for him. Jo looked up and saw a frosted bubble over each table.

"There must be security cameras up there," she thought.

Her father arrived into the room accompanied by a guard. He walked over, alone. Without sitting down, he lit into her in a low whisper, with a tirade of accusations.

"Unbelievable."

"You little ingrate."

"Just look what you've done."

"This is all your fault."

"No," Jo cut in, noting that at least one guard was starting to stir.

Jo spoke slowly and deliberately, like a teacher repeating a concept just beyond the grasp of a dull school boy. "This is completely your own fault."

"You are in prison," she explained. "For breaking the law. Child rape is illegal. People who do this, especially people stupid enough to film it, go to jail."

"For God's sake, shut up!" he hissed back. "People in here don't take well to hearing the specifics."

From then on, during her weekly visits, the two stuck to a script.

Once he was escorted into the visitor's room, she'd lay down the napkin of quarters in front of her on the table. He knew he couldn't touch it. He would indicate an item out of the vending machine, careful to stay behind the blue tile. She'd make the purchase, microwave his choice, usually a burger, and bring it back to the table for him with a cold Pepsi.

He'd say. "It's chilly–or, with the changing seasons, snowy or rainy or a little hot–today."

She'd say. "Yeah."

He'd say. "How's your mother?"

She'd reply. "Fine, I guess. I haven't talked to her."

At this point he'd lament. Jo would pass the time by categorizing the complaints in her head and cataloging them by number. After a three complaint combo–later she'd tell Francis it was, say, "a 27-2-11 today"–Jo would stand up and say, "I've got to go."

At this point he'd remark. "I got the deck of cards." and then request something else. "Hey, would you mail me some warm socks."

"We all want things," she'd say and be gone.

Spin the Plate

She and Francis never spoke much on the drive there, except for a brief interchange once they were outside the city with Jo insisting to pay to fill-up the tank with gas. Francis protested, once to the point where she pulled over and threatened to go by bus. Jo suspected a tank of gas would cost all the money Francis had to his name, a suspicion confirmed by the fact that when he picked her up each week the remaining quarter tank of gas was used, and the car was running on empty.

Between 20 and 25 minutes after arriving at the prison, Jo and Francis would turn back to the city. And, with Jo no longer tense and distracted, Francis would start up with, "Did I ever tell you about…"

Visiting her father drained Jo. Francis drove, and Jo closed her eyes and listened as he told his tales. Francis' favorite themes were wealth and power and their use and mis-use.

"Did you read the latest Mitchem novel?" he began, even though she'd told him before the last book she'd read was in high school English.

"The premise is that the obscenely rich can purchase anything at all. Taking it to the extreme, some of the wealthiest people in the world have extended their life spans to almost double the normal human lifetime. They used to buy up teenaged children from places like West Africa to harvest their organs, but now, if you can finance it, you can create as many exact genetic matches as you want. These clones are lobotomized from birth to make their caretaking more manageable and to make a direct transfer from a live donor possible. Of course, I wouldn't do anything like that, myself. I'll take my 70-90 on earth and then take my chances with the After."

"Privacy is another commodity that, with a little ingenuity, can be purchased. Limited layers is the key to privacy. That, and the right people in the right roles and responsibilities. Also, adaptation so that any loss in the structure triggers a pre-planned and immediate restructure to the network. Only the puppet master, who in a wealthy family is transitioned from parent to child, understands the entire network or even that there is a network beyond the layer below and above. One key unit is the front man, usually an actor. Reagan is the most obvious and famous example. But it doesn't pay to go so high profile. A better pick would be, say, a budding community theatre actor, a high school student in his sophomore year, typically the class president to groom into the position. He knows nothing of the identity of the puppet master as there is a layer separating him; he, of course, doesn't even realize how many layers exist. The puppet master has the final word on all his major decisions. He writes the front man's speeches too, though they come out sounding much better after a few rounds with editors and in the puppet's booming voice. Extreme charisma and public appeal, rare characteristics to begin with, don't seem to be traits inherent to those who are truly gifted and exceptionally skilled in politics or philanthropy. Or perhaps those other-directed tendencies atrophy over time with the adoration and acolytes of the masses."

Jo liked to listen to Francis go on. His voice rose and fell increasing in speed and animation.

"Haven't you ever thought it was strange in our country," Francis asked not requiring a response. "That those in positions of the highest power are so very normal? Whereas, on the other hand, creative geniuses are socially awkward by nature."

He elaborated. "The irony is that what appeals is the blandness of complete conformity to the popular thought, behavior, and beliefs of the day, devoid of passion and offensive to no one. Take someone like me. Imagine if I were to go to an Arab country, or even a political banquet right here in the US, spouting Jesus-loving slogans, and once served regional delicacies or simply steak and potatoes, pulled out an apple and a jar of peanut butter. It would be a public relations nightmare."

"The general public has a miniscule tolerance for oddities, passions, or any sort of original ways of acting, looking, or thinking. Anyone who is brilliant, passionate, and represents himself–a Lincoln, a King, Jesus himself–is met with teeth gnashing and almost certain assassination."

Basking in the comfortable warmth of the car heater, her mind occupied by Francis' endless stories, Jo felt tension she didn't realize had been gripping her slip away. She relaxed into the passenger's seat for the long ride home.

As it turned out, the prison sentence was not nearly as long as expected. After eight months, Jo's father was diagnosed in the prison infirmary with inoperable stomach cancer. Three weeks later, he was dead. A month later, Jo's mother died.

According to family folklore, Michaela became distraught after the death of her husband, disinterested in living, and had stopped eating. In truth, both her mother's emaciation and ultimately her death were a direct result of living alone for several months without anyone to lock up the liquor cabinet.

Jo reacted to her father's death as she always suspected she would. Much like anyone who's given prolonged care to a demanding, ungrateful family member, she felt the lifting of a great burden. She had fulfilled her role as dutiful daughter to the end and been the only person not to desert him, the only one by his bedside when he exhaled his final breath in morphine-induced peace.

Her mother's death however, smashed through Jo like an emotional tidal wave. Jo was about to shower for work when she received the call. "Very sorry... We'll know more after the autopsy...Neighbor called police... Newspapers piling up. You'll need to make a positive identification."

Jo immediately retreated to the privacy of her bedroom taking only Ben for comfort. He leaned into her as she pressed her face into his velvety shoulder. She choked on huge, dry sobs one on top of the other punctuated with primal screams.

Michaela had deserted her from an early age, limiting mothering strictly to providing a spotless house, freshly laundered clothes, and balanced meals. Unlike her father, her mother did not ask her for any sort of assistance and thwarted all attempts Jo made to reach out to her.

Jo thought back to an incident when she was 11 or 12 years old. She was home alone after school. Her mother was out shopping. Jo wanted to surprise her by vacuuming the living room just as her mother did every afternoon, first vacuuming at a 45 degree diagonal starting in the far corner. She was just finishing the second pass, vacuuming in perpendicular strips each overlapping the previous by a quarter of its width, when her mother bustled in. She took only enough time to settle the shopping bags on the counter before grabbing the machine from her daughter's hands with the customary, "Oh Juliana."

How the hell do you vacuum wrong?

The flash of anger was quickly replaced by a deep sorrow and then a growing chasm of guilt. Why hadn't she been checking on her mother? Why didn't she stop her father from hurting her? Maybe she wanted to pay her mother back for letting him hurt her? She knew. Yet, she let him beat her mother. She was no better than her mother.

She gulped a few breaths and then picked up the phone and dialed *1.

As the phone rang Jo realized that while Ben was a

good listener, she could count on Francis for making sense of complicated things.

"Talk to me," she choked out.

"What happened? Where are you?"

"Home."

"Do you need me to come there? What happened? Are you all right."

"I'm all right. I've done something terrible."

"What's going on?"

"My mother is dead. You know she was an alcoholic. I wasn't there for her. I let him beat her. I did nothing."

Francis sensed from her halting speech that Jo needed some time.

"Can I tell you about a strategy I made up. I use it when there's a thing too horrible to process or something's gnawing away at me."

Listening to Francis' rhythmic voice steadied Jo's breathing. She laid down on her back the short way across her bed with her legs hanging over one side. She closed her eyes sandwiching the phone between the bed and her ear and stroked Ben absently.

"I do what I call a 'plate spin,'" Francis told her. "...umm, it's sort of a fresh way of considering the situation, maybe armed with newfound knowledge or understanding, seeing through another's view point, or taking a broader time frame. Do you have time for a story?"

"Yeah."

"The plate spin idea is something I picked up from a sermon our deacon gave. It had such an impact that I asked him to email it to me."

Spin the Plate

Francis paused a moment while he withdrew a worn piece of paper from his wallet and unfolded it.

"The main point of the sermon was something about a pastor coming to terms with our deacon being at once both a minister and a solider, but let me read the part that stuck with me. He says, 'One evening I was having dinner with my wife's family. My nephew asked his father to place some ketchup on his plate. 'Daddy, put some ketchup right here' pointing to a spot on his plate. His father squirted a blob of ketchup on the left hand side of his son's plate near his French fries, at which point my nephew screamed, 'No! Not there, here.' as he pointed to the spot where he wanted the ketchup. Nothing seemed to work to get my nephew settled down. He just kept pointing to the spot. His father calmly reached over and spun my nephew's plate around one hundred eighty degrees so that the ketchup was placed at the exact spot my nephew kept pointing to. Then all was well. It was a matter of perspective.'"

"So what is the plate spin for you?" Francis said to Jo, getting to the point.

"God gives us the ultimate freedom," he went on, "which is the right to choose our own path in life without His interference. In this country we get to choose who to marry and whether or not to stay with them. Your mom made a lot of what I would consider bad choices especially when it came to your father. She was a rigid person who never waivered from those choices. When she was freed of your father, it appears she chose a path of further self destruction."

"Okay, how's this for your plate spin. You could

have sent your mother to prison. Active Concealment is a serious crime. Instead, when you were strong enough, you rescued her from your father and put an end to the beatings. You know Jo, you can't live someone else's life for them. The best you can do is provide them an opportunity to live it themselves."

In the lull that followed, Francis automatically slipped into silent prayer.

Jo felt the black chasm that was grasping her start to loosen its hold. She waivered on whether to voice her crime. She was tired of secrets.

"I should have done more."

Francis responded. "Your mom was a toxic person in your life. It wasn't good for you to interact with her. Cutting off ties was one of your protections and an important one. And you know, Jo, even when you attempted, she never allowed you to help her."

Jo insisted. "But after my father was put away, things might've been different. I thought there'd be more time. I never even tried."

"Ah," Francis said. "That is where forgiveness comes in."

"It's our nature as human beings to fall short," he began. "Whether or not anything you did here qualifies as 'falling short' is not for me to say. But I do know that all of us are fallible beings by nature. And it is by constantly turning to God, handing over our shortcomings and wrongdoings to him, and asking forgiveness, that we're restored and renewed. He's holding the offer of forgiveness out to you. You only need to accept it."

"Not yet," Jo responded. And then, "Crap. Keisha

is going to have a fit."

Francis said. "Do you want me to call her?"

"Yeah. Tell her I'm going to the morgue."

"I'll meet you there."

"No. Just tell Keisha I'll come in as soon as I can."

"Hang in there Jo-Jo," was all Francis could think to say.

CHAPTER 7: Lazy Sundays

After Jo's parents were laid to rest, a new Sunday routine emerged. Francis arrived early, at about 11:00 am. Today, he brought a medium-sized, cardboard U-Haul box. It was obvious that he had taken the message written on the side "This Box is Designed for Multiple Uses" to heart. Whatever the well-used box held was heavy. When Jo questioned Francis about it he told her, "I'll show you later."

Jo was still in her nightshirt. Nothing was rushed. She switched on the radio, clicked a preset button, and WROR's Sunday morning jazz played. Francis made coffee and apple pancakes, omelet burritos, multi-grain toast, and breakfast sausage links for Jo.

Francis always came brimming with stories, ideas, and questions. It seemed to Jo that he stored them up the whole week and they came spilling out during their Sundays together. It was as though he was starved for conversation. Political novels and newspaper stories were his passion. Not the kidnap, murder, death, destruction, sports, or finance pieces, but those with the common theme of compassion and hope for the desolate or forgotten. Every week he'd launch into a new story with a "Have you heard…" And usually she hadn't. Jo didn't own a television, and only recently had she become motivated to part with $1.50 for the daily newspaper.

She'd started over the past several weeks to pick up a paper at the T-station, leaving it in the back room at work and paging through the international and local sections during her break. She had stopped by the used bookstore near the shop a couple of times, too. She needed to remember to write down the authors and titles of the books Francis recounted each week. The sale clerk hadn't been able to help her find them from plot line descriptions alone.

"Have you heard of the initiative that is starting up in Sierra Leone?" Francis said as he browned the onions, garlic, and peppers in a thin layer of olive oil for breakfast burritos. He prefaced the story with a brief background of the culture, the history, the people.

"Sierra Leone is a country at the western most point of West Africa along the Atlantic Ocean. It's a little smaller than Maine and home to about six and a half million people. The official language is English, which is taught in schools. But most children can't afford to attend: though elementary school is free, the cost of uniforms, books, and supplies puts it out of reach for most families. There is no support for the orphans at all–most live on the streets, begging and panhandling for enough to eat. While those fortunate enough to get an education speak English fluently, the vast majority still speak Krio, a mix of English and several African languages."

"Sierra Leone should be a very wealthy country. Did you see the movie Blood Diamond?"

Jo shook her head.

"It's about Sierra Leone. Even though the country is rich in diamonds and other minerals, these natural recourses are under the control of outside companies and a handful of the very rich within Sierra Leone. The people only have to look around them to see that the government doesn't have their best interest at heart. Government corruption was one of the main reasons their decade long civil war started: a war that ravaged the country in every way possible. The situation is disheartening, and the poverty is enough to make you want to cry."

"There's this man who saw the movie and wanted to see the country for himself, firsthand, and meet its people. He's a writer. And a philanthropist, too. Once he arrived, he quickly discovered there are really only two classes in Sierra Leone: the extremely rich and the very poor. Yes, there's a small middle class, but in most countries they would be considered among the poorest. As the man drove through the country, his driver talked about how there was no hope for Sierra Leone, saying it was a country with no future. His own hope was to someday have enough money to move to the United States. Sadly, escaping Sierra Leone to the United States or England seems to be the dream of most of the poor there. The driver, who drove for visiting Americans, was considered middle class. His wife was employed as a registered nurse and made a salary of thirty dollars a month. They lived with their two boys in a shack with no running water or electricity and sacrificed all they had to keep their children in school. They were the lucky ones."

"It's no surprise that Sierra Leone is one of the

lowest-ranked countries in the world on both the Human Development Index and the Human Poverty Index. Even though the 10 year civil war has been over for several years now, the capital city of Freetown still looks like a war zone. The country is too poor to rebuild. Most government offices have their own generators, since power goes out just about every afternoon. And even the most basic of needs aren't satisfied. Anyone visiting is careful to buy bottled water from a reputable store, while the population gets their drinking water from streams and rivers. A well is a prized thing and is out of the reach of most people and villages."

"One day, as the man's car was stopped by traffic, a woman street vendor came up to his window. She asked if he would buy her some water. In the streets of Freetown cloudy water gathered from polluted streams sells in baggies for a few cents. He purchased her one of these small bags of water, thinking she would drink it down. She carefully took a few sips, and then retied the bag slipping it into her pocket. Clearly, this drink would be treasured with each mouthful savored as if it were 1961 Dom Perignon."

"During his trip, the man visited the home of a woman he had met there. It was during the rainy season, and the red dirt had been turned to muck. As he was returning to his car his feet and legs became splattered with red mud. When he had reached the passenger-side door, he heard someone calling his name. He turned and saw the woman he had just visited, running after him. She held a small bowl of water and a rag. When he faced her she immediately dropped to her knees and started washing his feet, ankles, and calves. His first thought was to take her shoulders and lift her up. Then he realized that she had nothing to offer him: not place to sit while they had talked, no clean drink, or cookies. This was her thank you, and it meant the world to her. When she finished and stood up, she searched his eyes wondering if he might be the answer to her prayers. Most of the way back to his hotel he couldn't help but to cry silently. Not just for this one woman, but for an entire nation lost in despair.

The next day the man had the chance to talk with a Sierra Leonean lawyer. The lawyer was a wealthy man with a most uncommon desire to help his fellow countrymen. The man shared with the lawyer what he had seen over the past few days and told him that his driver felt there was no hope for Sierra Leone. The man expected this Sierra Leonean lawyer to challenge the words, and tell him that things would change. But he didn't. He too felt that there was no hope. His prediction was bleak: within ten years, he told the man, Sierra Leone would be flung back into civil war.

"Nothing has changed," he stated. "And nothing will change here."

It was sad to learn that the one thing that both the rich and poor seemed to have in common was their hopelessness for the future of Sierra Leone.

"But you know Jo, as is the case pretty much universally, women are the keepers of the key to the salvation of their peoples. These women in Sierra Leone, if they just had a bit of seed money, could completely change not just their own life, but their families' and the village. There's this one program called 'Give a Little.' It provides funding for these women, just enough for a small herd of pygmy goats and a fence, a tiny fishing boat, or a sewing machine and some material. Then, they use the profits to buy more goats, fishing nets, or more material. A twist to *Give a Little* is that the receiver is asked to give back whatever they were given, so they contribute to someone else the first batch of kids, you know baby goats, to start their own little herd. Or a woman with a sewing machine is asked to time-share in the evening and night-time until another earns enough to get her own machine. The whole process is tracked on a wooden map in the center of the village, using colors and symbols, so a woman can see how her herd has propagated to the other families throughout the village and eventually beyond their village to a neighboring one. The intense poverty is not the biggest problem facing this country, you know; it is the despair that comes with utter hopelessness knowing full well that there is no way out. When these women see their impact, they become empowered, some even to pursue formal education for a son or daughter."

Francis poured the beaten egg mixture into the skillet, grated fresh parmesan on top, and warmed a tortilla in a second skillet.

"Once these techniques have been piloted and proven, a new initiative will kick off to draw the richer countries, more specifically US citizens, into the lives and plight of the peoples of the third world. With technology and the Internet, the world is shrinking, Jo. The two major barriers to effective involvement–our ability to just ignore what is going on and the ability of those in power to act corruptly–are being dismantled. The time is ripe in Sierra Leone as some in the new government are striving to create jobs and end endemic corruption. As long as we keep our distance from diamond mines and other mineral resources, and those in power share in a percent of the profits, we are increasingly being allowed to bring camera crews into the country."

Francis laid out the breakfast out on the table.

He said to Jo. "Mangia. Eat. Don't let it get cold."

Using jelly jar lids as miniature dishes, Francis fixed a breakfast for each of the rats and slipped into the spare room for a moment. He placed the tiny plates, one to every corner of the cage, so that each of the boys could put his back to the others, sit up on his haunches, and enjoy a meal to himself without fear of being accosted by a brother rat.

Francis fixed himself some peanut butter toast and as an after thought slipped an apple pancake onto his plate. He cautiously bit into the crust and shuddered slightly at the fruit's mushy texture. He chewed, noting it tasted like white bread but a bit sweeter, warm and appley, and swallowed.

"So, why don't people who have, give to those who don't?" he continued. "They are too far removed, and the act of giving returns no appreciation and little satisfaction. But imagine this. Imagine taking a small village and, with the consent of villagers of course, setting up multiple bank accounts: one for the town itself, one for the school and teachers, the hospital, and the police presence. There will also be bank accounts for neighborhoods each represented by a hand-picked family, one that meets the right criteria–hardworking, engaging, articulate, and most important, community minded. Funds donated to televised families would be shared with neighbors and their community as a whole so that off-air families are motivated to support their success."

"Then you create a reality-TV meets telethon program by setting up cameras everywhere. You have crack reporters to run interviews and two teams of talented television writers and editors working in tandem 24-7 merging together clips and stories. With about a 12 hour time delay everything that happens in their daytime is condensed into 40 minutes and then presented in an hour television slot, with commercials, the next day. It will be an every day soap opera of sorts, but participatory."

"The audience, to some degree, gets to determine the outcome as they contribute the amount and decide the distribution of income. They get to know the people and the town–which start out in desperate poverty–watching their stories unfold. The audience calls the various phone numbers to give, say, $8 toward the village well, $5 to the Ansumana family, $10 to the hospital. Families are then able to work their way out of their plight and further their community, with the hope that those families in the greatest need, the most industrious, and deserving will be rewarded with increased funding."

"On the giving end there is a degree of satisfaction and on the receiving side accountability, as both parties know just how the resources are used. Once a village hits a critical point of self sufficiency, the cameras and crew move to the next area and return annually for a follow-up television special and telethon. If the television show becomes popular, we could even create an on-line version in which people donate a one hundredth of a cent per-click as they try to make their own simulated Sierra Leone Fishing Village or Farm Town prosper."

"American Idol volunteered to do a pilot of sorts for the idea. If we could televise the plight of the third world and bring their reality into our living rooms, people would respond. The show raised over 50 million dollars in one night by showing the stark contrast between living conditions in the US and West Africa and showcasing real kids that needed help."

"American Idol. Is that the singing or dancing one?" Jo asked with a hint of distain.

"You've never seen American Idol?" Francis said incredulously. "Wait. Bring your breakfast into the living room."

Jo complied. Francis headed for the front door entry way.

"So anyways," Francis told her excitedly carrying his U-Haul box and setting it down on coffee table. "The basic gist is that music critics Randy, Simon, and Paula Abdul–she's a former pop singer and Laker's cheer leader–so the three of them audition about 100,000 people from around the country and pick about 100, which is where we are now. They'll get it down to the top 24. From that point on, people who watch the show live call in to vote for their favorites. The contestants with the lowest number of votes have to leave the competition. A lot of popular singers have gotten their start this way."

"It sounds absolutely," Jo was searching for the right word. "Freaking ridiculous. Why do you watch such crap?"

Francis said nonchalantly. "It's a good way to keep up with the pulse of US culture."

Jo raised her eyebrows at the obvious enthusiasm with which he unpacked the combination television and VCR from the box.

"Okay," he admitted. "I'm completely addicted to the show and a week behind."

What Francis neglected to tell Jo was that he had gotten to know Simon Fuller, the producer, and Simon Cowell, the British know-it-all judge, during taping of a benefit show in Sierra Leone. It was Francis who underwrote the expenses for Idol Gives Back which turned a profit fifty times what was spent two years in a row. Only very astute speed readers would have caught "The Saint Francis Foundation," a required legal claim, on the credits as they scrolled by at the end. Even the Simons did not realize fully Francis' involvement; they knew Francis only as one of the assistant writers on the set.

Francis said eagerly. "Okay, watch. I'll spare you the entire six hours I've got taped and fast forward past the initial auditions where people sang without music. Some were very good and others were a little, well, out there."

Francis advanced the tape to the first round filmed in Hollywood, where the performers sang in groups of three intermixed with solos showcasing the voice of each. The first four song choices were Sugar Pie, Honey Bunch; Do Wa Ditty; Midnight Train to Georgia; and Piano Man. Piano Man was sung by three Midwesterners. The trio had been out sightseeing the night before and sang notes very different from what was being played on the piano.

Randy said that it didn't work for him and that it was all over the place and pitchy. Paula said they looked great and she especially enjoyed their selection of coordinated leather boots; she wrinkled her nose and shook her head sympathetically, though, when it came to their music. Simon said the show wasted the money on their plane tickets to Hollywood and added the performance was a "complete embarrassment."

Jo listened politely, confirming her distaste for American culture. She was amused watching Francis, now perched on the wide arm of her recliner, and hearing his color commentary on the show.

Then after Francis by-passed the commercials came the next group: Dane, a six foot-four hunk with a heart who worked in the oil fields in Oklahoma; Maria from New York City, a Hispanic who was full figured, heavy, but not obese; and Treena, a woman who was about Jo's height and weight but lacked a muscular build. Treena was a dog groomer at PetSmart and a brief clip of her shaving a curly black cock-a-poo played during her intro.

"Great, they're going to made fun of the fatties," Jo thought. It was obvious to her that the show matched up these two women with the eye candy just to make it more embarrassing. Rehearsal footage played of the two women singing backup, but not insync.

"Francis, I really don't want to watch this," Jo said grabbing for the remote, but not sure what button to press to turn off the TV. Before she could figure out how to work the device, the musical number began.

The threesome sang the first notes to Billy Joel's The Longest Time. On stage was a piano and a cello, but just the cello accompanied to start.

The words flowed in sweet sounding three-part harmony. "If you said good bye to me tonight."

Jo stopped fiddling with the remote and glanced up at the trio on the screen.

Then Treena did the chorus flourish. "There would still be music left to write."

Maria jumped in with. "There's nothing I could do."

And Dane's part followed. "I'm so inspired by you."

Treena sang. "That hasn't happened."

Then the three of them. "For the longest time."

When they finished, Randy said to the trio. "Best performance of the night and one of the best I've seen." He called out Treena by name. "Treena, you can really sing. You owned that stage. Dane. Maria. 100% great job."

Paula Abdul agreed and said the song choice was perfect. She commented that the women looked beautiful and she meant it. Treena and Maria soaked it in.

"Dane," Paula said kiddingly. "You clean up okay."

Dane smiled humbly, knowing full well it was his

luck in song partners not looks that saved him from elimination.

And then, the moment of truth. Simon Cowell. He started by saying he was worried in the intro, but they worked it out. And then. "You have shown the others what talented singers sound like. I agree with Randy. One of the best I've seen. Treena, I know this is week one, but you have the makings of a star."

The fellow Idol contestants gave them a standing ovation, but their singular collective thought showed clearly on their faces. "Crap."

The camera zoomed in on Treena, glammed with a new hairdo and nice clothes and a broad smile.

Jo's eyes were fixated on the TV.

"That was interesting," she said trying to sound noncommittal. "Will they sing again?"

"Not until next week."

"Do you have that one?" Jo was hooked and not happy about it.

"No, but let's watch the end of this episode."

Jo agreed, but only so that she could scout out Treena's competition.

With Jo absorbed in the show, as was his habit, Francis pulled out his cell phone, clicked "Simon C" from his contacts, and typed a quick text.

"My gf liked your pick of Treena & thinks you're right."

As pompous as Simon Cowell appeared to be on television, he enjoyed flattery as much as anyone and looked forward to Francis' unbiased feedback each week.

Francis' phone beeped, and Jo grabbed it playfully.

"Hmmm…who are you texting?"

She punched a key. His Outbox message displayed on the screen.

"What's gf," she said accusingly. "Obviously it doesn't stand for 'good fuck' and it better not be the other thing."

Francis felt the back of his ears starting to redden and fumbled for words to say before it spread. "That's text language. It's just shorthand. Anyhow, do you want to watch the rest of that week's show?"

A sixteen year old boy with shoulder length hair was singing the chorus of Neil Diamond's Sweet Caroline with the audience shouting back. "So good, so good, so good."

Jo grabbed the remote and this time was successful in hitting pause. "gf stands for girl friend. You're bragging to your buddies that I'm your girlfriend."

"I was just texting. I was saving keystrokes," Francis protested.

Jo shook her head slowly back and forth, hit play on the remote control, and returned her gaze to the television screen.

The teen heartthrob crooned. "Warm. Touching warm. Reaching Out. Touching me." The audience erupted. "Touching you."

The boy singer continued. "Sweet Caroline."

The audience responded. "Oh, oh, oh."

This time it was Francis who hit pause. "Well are you?"

Jo sneered a little. "You are such a messed up little dude."

Francis parried. "Well, are you?"

Jo rolled her eyes. "Fine. But you're still not getting any sex."

Francis hit play on the VCR remote control to watch the rest of show. Then he shifted from the arm of the chair and squeezed next to Jo in her oversized recliner. She sidled over a bit to make room for him. He felt her body relax into his, and his heart soared. With his left hand he quickly turned off his cell phone and slipped it back into his pocket, before Jo could see the new incoming text message from "Simon C."

It read. "So you finally saw it. Of course I'm right."

Followed by another message. "Call me about flight to Freetown."

After the show, Jo lingered over a fresh cup of coffee and remained in her chair while Francis packed up the electronics. Jo studied him carefully. She turned over in her mind the phrase "my girlfriend" and then considered the flipside of the phrase: "my boyfriend." A boyfriend. Weird. But kind of nice.

Jo used to dread Sundays and the expansion of unplanned time; it was an especially bad day for remembering the past. But with Francis, she seemed to do a million things in a Sunday, yet the time raced by. Even before she had put a name to it, she knew that over the last several months they had evolved into more than just friends.

Again she rolled the phrase "my boyfriend" over in her mind, which was starting to drift. She was irritated with herself for wandering into a state she associated with not being in control. But the sensation was enticing. She succumbed to the tingling in her stomach, warm saliva in her mouth, a feel of floating, not tied to body, daydreaming, drifting. She thought about Francis and how his hair began to uncurl when he was overdue for a haircut, she thought back to him lying asleep on the sidewalk against IA, waiting for their first date, watching him sleep for a minute and then, when she nudged him with her foot, how he leapt up, so eagerly. She reflected on how he never bothered to hide how he felt and the easy smile he wore whenever he was with her. She thought how he smelled, the ever-so-faint scent of Jake cologne, and remembered he told her once that it was a graduation gift that he used sparingly and only for very, very special occasions. And she realized every time she saw him he smelled of Jake. She thought of how being near him calmed her, and she felt a sudden craving for his touch massaging her in the space between her ear and the back of her neck, as the tingling sensation in her midsection moved lower.

"I remember the first time I saw your face," Jo ventured. "I thought you were a graduate student in a Bohemian stage."

"And now....well..." she admitted. "You're not so bad to look at."

Francis left his electronics and went to Jo.

"The first time I saw your face, I thought you were the most beautiful woman I had ever seen," Francis confessed.

"Don't mess with me," Jo was now uncomfortable.

"No. It's true. I'm normally not the stalking type, but I staked out the late morning D line for over a month, watching you from a distance on those days when you took the train before I finally got up the nerve to ride the same car and introduce myself. I'd go home and tell my aunts about you at night. To tell you the truth, I think when they first met you they assumed we'd had more than just the one date. You know, Jo, I meet new people every single day, and the greed, indifference, shallowness, and cruelty I see, well… most of them sicken me. Sometimes I want to die, just to get away from the human race. I didn't think such a person existed: someone genuine, passionate, and compassionate. You are a pearl of great value. The moment I saw you I thought you were the most beautiful thing I had ever seen, and now I know it's true."

The sincerity in Francis' voice left no room for Jo to doubt that he fully meant everything he said. She allowed herself to look him in the eye and when she did, neither could turn away. Francis slowly lifted his hand and gently trailed his fingers along Jo's cheek, then traced her jawline. Jo automatically stiffened, but their eyes were still locked. Jo was overwhelmed. She had no idea how to respond. She felt the muscles of her face involuntarily starting to relax.

Francis knew it would still be sometime before Jo could fully trust him. He sensed she was torn about his touch, so he smiled. Then lowered his hand.

Francis said to her. "Tell me something. About you."

Jo didn't want to disappoint him, but really what was there to tell?

"Sundays are good. But otherwise, every day is pretty much the same; sometimes I feel like it runs into one long day."

Francis pleaded. "Come on. Share one feeling." The eagerness with which Francis drank in even the smallest tidbit of information encouraged her to say more.

Jo said. "Fine. This guy came in a few weeks ago and wanted a crashed Kia Sorrento on his back. He brought me a picture and asked if I could do it for him. I said yes, but it would take a long time, and it would cost a lot. He gave his American Express card which he told me had no limit."

"So I did the crashed car on his back, in layers, over a few times. And then when I was done, he asked me if I could put writing underneath and I said sure. He said 'great.' And told me to write 'Jimmy 1992 to 2009.' Turns out that was his baby brother who was killed by a drunk driver. He was hoping that there'd be one person who'd see it and think twice about driving shit-faced."

"So, what did you feel?" Francis wondered

"Pain. My hand hurt after all that work."

"Com'on," Francis said.

"And I felt sad. Yeah. Sad. A little jealous too that this Jimmy had a big brother to look out for him, even though at the end he wasn't able to. See. I just shared a feeling."

"Oh yeah, I got a cat yesterday," Jo informed him.

Francis commented. "Another one?"

Jo explained. "I stopped by the shelter…"

Francis continued for her. "…and you were strolling down death row and heard a cat yowl, 'dead feline walking.'"

Jo admitted. "Sort of. On the side of his cage read 'Shy, not good with children or dogs, needs to be an only cat.' From the markings on the note I could see they planned to declaw him, probably as a last resort. Stripping away his defenses would be the worse thing in the world for an animal like that. So, he came home with me."

Francis was curious. "What did you name this one?"

Jo said. "Bagheera."

"The black panther from the jungle book." Francis noted. "What's he like?"

"He's very timid and, right now, if you push him he hisses and claws."

"How do you feel about this one?"

"I feel like a sap. See, I shared another feeling."

Laughing, Francis got up and headed towards the kitchen.

"He just needs to discover his inner panther," Francis said. Soon he was elbow deep in soapy water.

"Pretty much," Jo said. And then. "Leave the dishes, I'll do them tonight."

Francis liked the sentiment, but knew Mount Dishes would be there waiting the following week. He didn't mind and said, "Thanks, but I'll take care of them. I never get to do any of this for myself."

He kidded. "You know I like my peanut butter and apples raw and served on a paper plate."

While Francis washed the pots and dishes, Jo looked through the "Local" section of the Boston Globe for something free for them to do. Francis insisted on paying for their Sunday outings, and Jo got the distinct feeling that he'd have to go without for the rest of the week as a result.

"All right," Jo announced. "Choices for today include balloon fest on the Common, American Gerbil Society show at the Cambridge Montessori School, the Harvard Museum of Natural History, or the Isabella Stewart Gardner Museum, which is free today because it's the first Sunday of the month."

"And we'd get to be Isabellas for a day," Francis proclaimed matter of factly.

"What?"

"Isabella Steward Gardner felt a bit out of place because there weren't a ton of Isabellas around. So, when the building, land, and paintings were donated to the city, it was with the stipulation that anyone named Isabella would get in free anytime."

"Really?" Jo wondered how any one person could hold onto so much useless trivia.

"Plus, one day a month the museum has to be open to the public–hence today we are all Isabellas."

"Let's go," Jo decided for them.

They headed out the door, the last of the dishes still soaking in the sink.

Though Jo was as absorbed as ever by her work, it seemed the weekdays passed much more slowly than they ever had before. And Sunday, her weekly day with Francis, flew by far too quickly. With each passing week, she could feel her façade dissolving slowly, so slowly, probably no one else would even notice. Except for Francis. Francis seemed to be aware of everything, especially when it came to Jo. Almost against her will, she began to trust him.

Several weeks passed since their first lazy Sunday at Jo's house. And every week Jo found a new no-cost activity; this week it was meandering through the Fenway Victory Gardens.

"This is the last Victory Garden in existence," Francis informed Jo as he filled his backpack with sandwiches, apples, and cookies.

"Richard D. Parker established the gardens to help with food shortages during World War II and then worked to preserve them as a historic landmark. He kept his own plot until his death. Today, anyone who wants to maintain a 15 by 25 foot garden, right in the heart of Boston, can."

They took the Green Line to the Symphony stop and, after a 10 minute walk, entered the garden from the Boylston Street entrance. Hundreds of weekend gardeners lovingly tended their cornucopia of plots brimming with flowers, herbs, and vegetables. After about an hour of admiring the abundant flora, Jo suggested that they find a spot for lunch.

Francis replied with a familiar line. "I know a place."

On the way, they came to a garden with a bush of huge red roses in full bloom at the entrance. Inside was a miniature labyrinth of paths with all kinds of vegetation. Francis approached the bush, stopped, and smelled one of the roses. He took out a pocket knife and expertly cut the rose from the bush leaving a long stem. Then he popped off the thorns and handed it to Jo. She knew she was supposed to be touched by the romantic gesture, but thought stealing roses was probably illegal, and worse, rude.

"I can't take this."

Francis stepped inside the garden and indicated for her to follow. He brushed aside some mulch in front of a foot tall gray ceramic St. Francis statue to expose a small plaque which had on it the inscription "Francis Mangini."

Jo smelled the rose, now that she knew it was legit, and gave him a quick, spontaneous hug. Her first rose.

"You have a Victory Garden," she said, stunned. "It must be a lot of work."

"Gosh, no. I'd never have time to do all this," said Francis.

"It's sort of a gift," he explained. "From a woman I helped out once. It was her way of saying 'thank you.'"

Jo's heart started to thump. "What did you do for her?"

Francis got that same evasive look on his face as when she asked about his job situation.

"It's a long story," he said vaguely. "She was at a cross roads in her life, and I made it possible for her to start down a new path. She insisted on giving me something. I suggested some flowers or a nice plant."

Francis gestured with a sweeping motion toward the garden and said. "She gave me this."

Jo felt the white hot flash she usually associated

with being challenged or threatened. She looked around her, confused. There was no one there. Except Francis. Francis with his talk of some woman.

"Wait," Jo wondered incredulously. "Could I be jealous?"

Just then, at the back corner of the garden, a tall woman arose from her knees and emerged from behind a tree-sized plant that had elephant-ear shaped leaves and rhubarb shoots every which way. The woman's rapid gait and regal posture belied her age. She was well-freckled, tanned, and fit. As she approached, Jo could see from the crows feet by her eyes that she was well past retirement. Jo's heart resumed its normal beat.

"Francis, darling. I thought I heard your voice," the woman said. She removed dirt smattered hardware grade gloves and leaned down a bit to kiss him on the cheek.

"You've brought a friend," she said.

"This is my girlfriend, Jo," Francis informed her.

At those words, the woman beamed and said. "My name is Valerie. It's wonderful to meet you. Jo, can I show you the garden?"

Valerie handed Francis a bottle of rust colored liquid that was near a line of new green bean shoots and asked if he would mind giving them a squirt. Then she took Jo by the elbow and headed into the garden.

Valerie never tired of touring her showpiece. As she spoke, it quickly became clear this was a science, as well as a labor of love.

"My father had a victory garden in the backyard in Roxbury when I was a little girl," Valerie began. "It

Spin the Plate

wasn't always a rough neighborhood, you know. I used to play outside alone in the garden, and it was perfectly safe. That garden produced wonderful vegetables, which we fertilized with our own compost. My father had a great distain for chemicals! I helped him make the compost of vegetable peelings, chopped leaves, wood ashes, and horse or cow manure. My father liked to grow tomatoes, green beans, and cucumbers that I remember. He always used hot sauce to deter rabbits and deer."

It made Jo wistful to hear the happy memories this woman still kept from a long ago childhood enjoying the solace of a garden together with her father.

When Jo's attention returned, Valerie had moved on to the more combative side of gardening. "You don't need to worry about squirrels–they usually won't eat in a vegetable garden. They go for tulips. There aren't deer in the Fenway, but rabbits, yes. They love carrot-tops, young green bean plants, beets, and also lettuce. You could come back one day to see your row of tender green bean leaves reduced to a row of 1 inch stems. A coyote took off with all the rabbits one year saving me much anguish. But he must have moved on or been removed; this year I've had baby rabbits fearlessly running through my plot. The hot sauce is watered down with two parts water and sprayed on while the leaves are just emerging. Though, I have to say it's hard to discourage rabbits after they've had a taste of something and they know where to look."

Valerie led Jo through a maze of beets, carrots, mesclun, zucchini, summer squash, and various herbs including parsley, thyme, oregano, sage, basil, chives, rosemary, and edible nasturtiums. She explained that she'd planted the marigolds along the garden edges to discourage leaf chewing bugs.

Jo was admiring a very orderly row of tomatoes in cone-shaped wire cages: cherry, beefsteak tomatoes for eating and roma tomatoes for cooking. She tried not to appear distracted. Jo didn't want to interrupt, but she had questions. Questions about Francis.

"So, anyway," with Francis out of earshot, Jo felt compelled to ask, "does Francis bring all his women here?"

Valerie laughed. She wiped her eyes. Then laughed some more at the thought.

"No," She replied. "You're it."

Valerie elaborated. "Francis comes here, alone, to weed the garden. And to think. He tells me that sometimes he just needs to get his hands dirty. He doesn't say much else."

That was a bit shocking for Jo to hear. When she imagined Francis it was either the image of him speaking or staring at her in eager anticipation for her response. A quiet, reflective Francis was a side of him she rarely saw.

"I haven't seen him or signs of his work here for some time," Valerie informed Jo. "With Francis' absence over the past year, I've put hay around my tomatoes and cucumbers: hay virtually discourages all weeds and keeps the need for watering down, too."

Then turning her attention from her beloved vegetation she confided to Jo. "I'm glad he's okay." And looking into Jo's eyes she added. "And that he's found someone."

Spin the Plate

After Francis' backpack was filled with a basket of fresh vegetables, herbs, and Jo's rose safely packaged, they said their goodbyes. And Jo and Francis continued on toward the lunch site.

They walked a little ways from the gardens and down a barely trampled path though some woods and arrived to a short climb up a steep cliff. Francis went first with Jo following right after. He scrambled up the precipice with surprising strength and agility.

Francis, making it to the crest, turned and reached towards her. Jo's first thought was to rebuff the outstretched hand. Or make a joke. Come on. Did he really think she couldn't make it on her own, that he somehow was going to haul her up, that she needed him? She hesitated, gazing skyward. He was illuminated by the sun behind him. God, he looked so beautiful. Her desire for him terrified her. Sometimes looks can deceive. She had to be cautious. One thing she knew: men were by nature apathetic, self-centered, arrogant, and callous. She considered the brilliant being before her: refined, courageous, steadfast. She slowly extended her hand to him. Their fingertips brushed. Her skin tingled at his touch; her body hairs stood on end as the sensation encompassed all of her. Without another thought, she kicked off against a rock with her right foot. In one fluid movement, Francis grasped her hand and drew her upwards.

In the next instant, Jo found herself seated beside Francis, his left arm still curled around a sturdy, young oak. A most amazing scene was laid out before them. Hundreds of victory gardens blanketed the ground below in a patchwork design. Each was its own little world. It suddenly occurred to Jo that there is the world you are thrust into and the world you create. Each gardener fashioned a private place. She and Francis, they too were developing a microcosm of their own making.

Looking around them it was obvious Francis was not the only one privy to this vantage point. The squirrels, while absent in the gardens, seemed to congregate here.

"It's all the acorns," Francis explained.

"But they really prefer these," he said, pulling a bag of roasted unsalted peanuts from his knapsack.

Jo wondered if he packed squirrel goodies every week. It would be like Francis, always busy and never rushed, to bide his time, peanuts at the ready, patiently awaiting the day she'd suggest a Victory Garden excursion. They devoured their sandwiches and tossed nuts to the cuddly rodents who became more bold and greedy with each nibble.

Jo was astonished at how friendly the squirrels were. She often tried to feed the squirrels in the tiny courtyard behind her apartment, but the Newton squirrels were afraid of people. So it was quite a surprise to see that Fenway squirrels had no fear. The boldest one practically took the peanut right out of her hand. At home it was such an effort to hand feed them: Jo was always trying to find ways of getting close without spooking the skittish creatures. Here, since there was no fear–and no challenge–she didn't hand over the peanuts right away, waiting to see what the squirrels would do. How far would they go? She followed their lead and let them work for each tidbit:

standing up, climbing on boulders and stumps, and coming real close to her. Jo suspected she could get this one squirrel to crawl on Francis' lap. Francis was fascinated, despite knowing full-well that wild rodents can harbor mites or lice, as the squirrel crept closer and closer. He could see the coat was not actually brown, but had a rust-colored under fur with black hair tips. The fuzzy face had fine, fanning whiskers and short, thick black eyelashes. Just as the squirrel put a tiny paw on Francis' knee, Jo relinquished the peanut. It was peculiar to see cute little wild animals actually trusting humans, and fun, as though they were in one of the old-style Disney animated films.

Upon returning to Jo's apartment a few hours later, Francis unloaded from his backpack the basket of vegetables and a plastic bag with two dozen empty soda cans and beer bottles he had collected. He peeled off the label from a green Heineken bottle, washed it thoroughly, and put the rose and an inch of water in it and set it on the kitchen counter. He gave the rest of the empties a quick rinse. Each could be returned for a five cent deposit.

"You need to learn to take a day off," Jo joked.

Francis smiled because it was funny and because he knew she wouldn't press further about his source of income. Jo was not one to pry, and the pained look on Francis' face whenever she approached the topic of his employment let her know to back off. Jo guessed that like so many others in this country right now, he was out of work and doing whatever it took to get by.

Jo took the dogs outside and upon returning she asked Francis to put them in her bedroom so she could let the rats run free. Muzzy was the first rat sprung loose and made a bee line for Francis. Muzzy had a special affection for Francis, which Jo secretly thought was due to his peanut butter breath. Francis settled into the bean bag chair. Muzzy crawled up on his chest, curling his head into the nook of Francis' neck, grinding his teeth in contentment, as Francis rubbed the animal's jaw and around his ears. After a time, Muzzy inched his way up toward Francis' face. Muzzy liked to give kisses, his soft velvety tongue tickling Francis' lips. If not dissuaded he would take it to the next level and pry open his mouth to floss out particles between his teeth.

"Jo," Francis pleaded. Jo arose from lying on the floor reading the comics. She dislodged the rat's head from within Francis' mouth and scooped him up tickling the small creature and blowing raspberries on his fuzzy belly, until he spun away, energized for a surprise attack on one of his brothers.

Jo moved into the comfortable, oversized chair and reclined. Francis followed her.

As usual, it began rather innocuously, as Francis would say, "Do you mind if I…"

Sometimes he would brush her hair, massage her hands, or rub her feet. What followed then was an increasingly sensual experience. Today, he started by brushing her hair with a metal comb. Next, he gently traced the length of her neck with his fingers, before kneading her shoulders. He worked his way down to her hands, giving soft bites and kisses in between the fingers.

She remembered his first touch: she had stiffened in his hands. Thinking back to herself then made her think briefly of Bagheera on the day she brought him home. Even then, as a scruffy black tom curled in the farthest corner of the cage hissing at her through glowering yellow eyes, it has been easy for her to visualize the animal as a sleek, enormous panther of a cat. Now, weeks later, he ruled the rescue/exercise room stretched across the length of her weight bench, tail swaying slightly and emitting swells of rumbling contentment as she walked by giving him a rub behind the ears.

Francis' touch was soft and sure. Jo had relaxed that first day after realizing she could send him flying across the room with one smack. And, if all else failed, there was always the gun handy. So, she had let him continue. Now, she awaited this part of their Sunday routine with fervent anticipation. She found he had a good instinct for her likes as well as a talent for reading her reaction to his touch. She developed a silent code, which she used to accelerate the learning. Communicating in black jack signals, Jo would tap (more) or rub (pass) the arm of her chair. After Jo had fallen into a deep relaxation under his touch, Francis would run hot water in the tub, placing bubble bath, bath beads, or oils and always lighting a candle in the same or complimentary scent. Then he would leave.

Today his departure left a deep void, an unfamiliar

longing. Jo lay in the warm bubbly water; her thoughts fixed on Francis. What would it be like if he didn't leave on Sundays. What if for once he stayed. She closed her eyes, draped one arm outside the tub, rested the other between her thighs, and imagined it.

Normally Jo would undertake an especially long, arduous Sunday evening workout. Instead, tonight, she put on a fresh night shirt and crawled under her covers. She was tempted to fall sleep, but terrified that the sense of tranquility would not last through the night. To compromise she set the alarm before lying down. Jo drifted to sleep imagining Francis holding her close with both of them satisfied and spent. She had the most restful nap since she was two years old. When the alarm rang at 11:30 pm she dressed and headed out for the city.

CHAPTER 8: Conversion

One Sunday evening Jo reclined in her chair with Ben stretched on top of her, his head resting on her shoulder, body laid across her chest and his tail curled beneath him in her lap. The dog sighed in contentment; it was a new experience, one that they both found enjoyable, for Jo to be awake and still.

Jo was preoccupied and mildly amused watching Francis absorbed in working out a knotty theological issue. Francis liked to cultivate ideas aloud. Jo listened without the typical, outside world response to his religious talk: a glazed-over look, forced politeness, or outright hostility. Void of any religious training or preconceptions and because she had no agenda or stake in the outcome, Jo came at it from a new angle and one which Francis found refreshingly direct.

Francis slowly traced the parameter of the room saying. "So, yeah, the switch occurred between Old and New Testament. Around the time of Job, God gets this idea, or probably we just evolved enough to be privy to the idea He always had. In either case Job represents the test case of how things are going to work from now on. God is and always has been excruciatingly slow, at least by our sense of time, to responding to the pain, suffering, and crying out of His people. But at least in the ancient times, the suffering was a direct result of disobeying God. In that sense, people deserved what they got. With Job, on the other hand, God allowed a lot of crap to happen for no apparent reason, through no fault of Job's own."

"The bright spot in this is that He uses the crap that happens to us or is done to us for something good. He turns it all around. This is just one example of God as revealed in the Old Testament, and later God incarnate as Jesus, as the ultimate Plate Spinner."

"Job's situation in particular represents a mega plate spin. No longer is it an eye for eye or follow the rules and get a blessing. The way He explains the new world order with Job's case is pretty simple. Job loses everything: belongings, livestock, servants, children, wives, his own health. Then, through Job's steadfast faithfulness, all is restored, plus more."

Francis added as he approached Jo. "Those were the good old days when you could trade in a wife, you know, upgrade."

Jo reached out smacked him as he passed.

"Ow." He protested, grinning. "But seriously. The message here has to do with suffering and sacrifice with a purpose: giving up something for greater gain. Sacrifice used to mean giving up a pigeon or a goat and gain was prospering in health and wealth. Now, the stakes are upped. Jesus demonstrated the ultimate sacrifice: giving up His own life with a hefty amount of suffering leading up to His death. The gain in His case was creating an entryway for salvation of the human race. Eleven of His twelve apostles followed suit, all similarly martyred."

Spin the Plate

"Yeah, it was pretty horrible–the apostle John was able to live out his life on an island, writing, after a botched attempt to boil him alive, but the rest of the Apostles were crucified, stoned, beaten to death, that sort of thing. Saints throughout the ages have suffered a variety of awful and similar treatments. Of course no one group has an exclusive on suffering. Persecution is the one manmade resource that always seems to be plentiful."

Francis' gaze settled upon Jo. "God, she's so beautiful," he thought. Jo stared at him intently waiting for him to continue his trail of thoughts. Francis strained to recall what it was he was talking about.

"Ah…suffering," he continued. He diverted his full attention on Jo.

"What about you? Your father molested you; your mother allowed it; your teachers looked the other way. But yet, as completely abominable and inexcusable as it was, if all of that had not been so, would you be who you are today? God often seems to grant powers to survivors not possessed by those cruising through life. Perhaps with you it is the longing to rescue and a fearlessness of the night, as well as just about anything or anyone else. There is a great power within that combination."

Francis alighted on the bean bag chair and from there considered Jo. "God loves you, you know."

At this point Jo cut in. "Stop with the 'L' word. You know that I hate that word. Why don't people just say what they mean?"

"Love, hah!" Jo shook her head in disgust. "I heard it all the time growing up. It sickens me when I overhear children, parents, friends, partners, or spouses say it now. Each time it means something else; and never a definition you'd find in the dictionary. I don't understand what it is supposed to mean, only what it does mean. People use the 'L' word to cover up something else, some sort of 'I want' or 'don't,' like 'don't leave me,' 'I want sex' or 'I'm working towards having sex sometime in the future,' 'I need you to say it back to me,' 'don't be angry,' 'don't hurt me,' 'don't be upset,' 'don't be in a bad mood,' 'convince me that I'm not unlovable.'"

Jo concluded. "Don't ever say that word to me or I may have to bust you up a little."

"Okay," Francis replied.

"And another thing," Jo retorted. "Obviously God does not 'love' me. How could He claim to and have let all that shit happen? Where was He? What was His role? What is He anyways, some sort of superhero on standby?"

Francis did not answer right away. He looked sad and troubled.

He finally spoke. "I would never question His judgment, after all He is God. But just between you and me, extending free will to everyone seems like a pretty crappy policy. So why didn't He reach down from Heaven, scoop you up in his arms, and smite your parents on the spot? Inflict your teachers with boils or frogs?"

Francis fell still and was silent again. Then he said. "I don't know why. If I were God, with all that power at my finger tips, there would be a lot more smiting."

Francis thought for a moment and then went on.

Spin the Plate

"God works in a different way. I guess I just don't know why. Why don't you ask Him yourself? And, listen. You'll get an answer. Or maybe peace knowing He's in charge and He's got it figured out."

Suddenly Francis leapt to feet, pacing, moving more rapidly now. "What about this."

Rufus raced over to join him. Francis didn't seem to notice the giant dog leaping at his side as he traversed the room in a walk so fast it was almost at a jog.

Francis said excitedly. "Think about it. Suffering, Sacrifice, Gain. Childbirth is a good example. When a woman has a baby, it is the painful labor that produces complete joy. She doesn't care about the pain, or at least accepts the pain, because she has the whole picture. Some women even do it all over again, knowing clearly that the pain is for a purpose, a reason, an end result."

"We hold this expectation, but with no foundation at all, that God will give His people an easy, pain-free life. It seems to be just the opposite. Many people who reject God are the ones living out cushy lives. Those who choose to serve may go through pretty horrific experiences. Clearly belonging to God doesn't mean living painlessly. But, the pain can lead to good, joyful, amazing, unbelievably incredible outcomes. Maybe it is even necessary."

Francis walked over to Jo, with Rufus still at his heels, knelt beside her and searched her face. "I have a question for you. What if you could sacrifice your own childhood so that others might have theirs? Would you do it?"

Jo thought briefly of the girls on the street and felt the familiar throbbing pang. She remembered the slight girl with silky black hair and dark almond eyes who she had protected one night and then left behind. "Maybe. Yeah, but no one asked me."

Francis said. "He didn't have to ask. He knew. What happened, what was perpetrated against you, was not good, not right, but perhaps the outcome is a burning desire to save others in similar circumstances, and the ability to make them listen and follow you out of there, because you know what it is like. You've been there too. A certain power comes with making it beyond a trauma and it having no hold on you, making it to the other side with no fear, no tears, not chained, and untouched: '*he walks through fire, yet he is not burned.*'"

Francis stood up and resumed a slow pace.

He sighed. "Oh, Jo-Jo, how would I know? It's all theories, ideas, speculation. I was born with a silver spoon in my mouth."

Jo thought it was a funny thing to say, but she let him go on and did not remind him of his parent's early death and his living in near poverty. Francis stopped completely, standing still. Rufus pawed at his side a couple of times, then plopped into a sit next to him, tongue lolling, and staring at his face.

More subdued, Francis said. "What could I know about real pain and betrayal? I've always just been given everything I need. I've never been brutalized or endured real suffering. Really. Do something for me, ask God if He would send you the answer. You ask Him for me. I know He will answer. Then explain it back to me."

Jo closed her eyes. The conversation tired her, but in a sleepy, not agitated, sort of way.

Opening her eyes, Jo said to him. "You are an excitable little man."

Then, more seriously, Jo admitted. "Francis, I'm tired."

She repeated deliberately. "I'm tired Francis."

He looked at her, head tilted. It reminding Jo of Rufus' quizzical look. Francis realized suddenly that he had never before heard Jo express even the smallest bodily need or desire.

"I can never rest, never stop, never relax, never let my guard down," she confided. "The only time I feel momentarily satisfied is when I'm looking for a fight or smashing someone in the face. I only sleep when I've brought my body to utter exhaustion."

Jo remarked. "You lost your parents when you were three. You own nothing. You struggle to make it through the week, and yet…"

"I have much more than you know," Francis told her.

Jo said. "I want it, too."

Francis paused for only a moment. He had been to enough conferences to know the place of the layperson in the church and the proper course of action. His role was to bring people into the church and have ordained ministers take over from there. He also knew a drawn-out, formal process of Jo's establishing a relationship with a priest or minister, joining a church, taking preparatory classes, receiving the sacraments, and so forth simply was not going to happen. He had had enough evangelical encounters that he thought he could wing it. And, he knew as clearly as he knew anything God's great affection and desire for this woman.

So, without missing a beat, Francis prayed for the right words and responded. "Do you want the Lord Jesus Christ to take on all your burdens and wash away your sins, for the Holy Spirit to enter into you, and to become a child of God for all eternity?"

Jo sighed loudly. "Okay." And stood up, leaving Ben in the recliner and approaching Francis.

Francis said. "You'd better sit down for this."

Jo sat cross legged on the floor. Francis knelt in front of her and put one hand on each shoulder. He spoke in a rhythmic chant, talking as if to an old friend. She closed her eyes and breathed deeply.

In the silence, he slowly inhaled and then expelled the air, matching his breathing to hers. In a sing-song voice, Francis prayed. "Oh Father God, magnificent in glory, unfailing in patience, who desires union with all your human creation. Jo comes to you earnestly seeking, yearning for reconciliation…"

He sounded very far away.

A crinkling sensation buzzed between Jo's ears, then she was hit with a rush of wind. As her arms went limp and head slumped forward, she was glad to be sitting. Eyes welled. Francis continued to chant. After some time, Francis fell silent. Jo opened her eyes, wet and shining with the whites a brilliant white.

"I think it took," she said.

And then. "So what now?"

Francis took a worn New Testament out of his

back pocket and handed it to her, saying, "This is a general guide–an instruction manual of sorts. I'll give you the first half next week. Pay attention. Listen. God has big plans for you. Are you baptized? You'll want to join a church. You may have to try a bunch to find the right flavor."

"I'm not a joiner," she said.

"Okay, whenever you are ready, then," he replied.

CHAPTER 9: Confession

After spending their Sundays together–and as Francis slipped out the door and Jo lingered in her oversized tub enveloped by hot water, bubbles, and the smell of lavender, cinnamon, or vanilla–Jo found she was increasingly left with a strange and unfamiliar longing. Jo craved the physical, human contact of his touch. No more just pretending.

This week, as Francis headed out, she said the word aloud to him.

"Stay."

"I want to," he replied. "You can't imagine how much I want to, but it's not a good idea."

"You know," Francis admitted. "Technically, I'm still a virgin."

"Ah…" Jo teased. "And technically you still live at home, with your aunts. So that makes you sort of a '40 Year Old Virgin' meets 'Failure to Launch.'"

Francis feigned insult. "No, 33 year old virgin, well 33 next Sunday. Hey, let me plan the day. There is something I've been wanting to ask you. I'll get your answer then. All I want is a 'yes' or 'no.' Don't give me anything else."

"I wasn't planning on it," Jo said.

Then, even though he didn't seem phased, she felt

Spin the Plate

a rare compulsion to explain herself and added. "I don't do gifts."

The following Sunday morning Jo lay awake in bed, resting. She didn't know who or what God was, but the experience she had at the moment of her conversion made her crave more of it, more of Him. Her mind traveled, not to the sad and scary, but to a thought that had hold on her. It was the concept of herself as an eternal being. The idea that the years on earth were a beginning in preparation for living forever consumed her. Lately when she loped through the city at night, she felt almost as though she were about to fly, as if only she could take a big enough stride she would propel herself forward with sufficient force to leave her body. That is what the afterlife was, she imagined, a leaving of this physical body for one with no ailments, pains, limitations, or needs: a body that no one could penetrate or abuse.

She heard the familiar brake squeal of Francis' Nova. She sprang out of bed, giving her teeth a quick brushing, and met Francis at the door, opening it before he could knock.

"Happy Birthday," she said.

"Yes, it is," he replied.

Looking outside for the first time that morning, Jo squinted in the bright light. It was a glorious Indian summer day. Francis stood in the doorway with a large picnic basket in one hand and holding a good sized cooler in the other. Francis wore a new white dress shirt and a purple patterned tie. After letting him in; Jo lifted the top of the cooler and discovered bottles of champagne and sparkling cider and two glasses.

"What are we celebrating?" she asked.

"That is to be determined. So, are you up for a surprise adventure?" he queried.

"Sure."

"Okay, we'll get going as soon as you're ready."

"Okay."

Francis grabbed a couple of plastic bags and took the dogs for a short walk through the neighborhood. When he returned he tossed the now full bags into a public trash can in front of Jo's apartment. He opened the back door of the Nova and said to Rufus and Ben, "Jump in." Francis helped himself to three generous squirts of Purell waterless hand sanitizer he kept in the glove compartment.

Jo met him at the door, this time dressed. After a quick rummaged through her closet, she had found a deep purple peasant-style mid-calf length skirt and matched it with a purple and yellow flannel shirt with the sleeves rolled and tied at the waist. And she put on her forgotten old-favorite Birkenstock slip-on leather beach sandals. She felt strange without the overalls as if she were out of uniform. Francis' lingering gaze and slowly spreading grin let her know he appreciated her attire. They put the basket and cooler back into the trunk. Francis opened the passenger door for Jo, and she found a large hot coffee "extra, extra" waiting for her in the cup holder. As Francis walked around to the driver's side, Jo noticed that the gas tank needle was pointing to full.

Francis made his way onto the Mass Pike West taking the Framingham exit; after miles and miles of contiguous strip malls, the view along Route 20 started to become more scenic. They drove through sleepy residential towns that were once mainly farmhouses and apple orchards.

Francis knew this was it. Now was the time. He took a deep breath and prepared for the speech of his life, one he had been practicing for months. A speech he would deliver himself.

He began slowly and calmly with the first sentence. "I need to tell you about myself: my job, what it is I do, what and who I am."

After just a few lines, his carefully memorized monologue abandoned him. But there was no stopping now. Francis' words tumbled in a rapid-fire free-flow.

"It started about two years ago with a dream. I dreamed of a warrior. I didn't want to introduce myself until I was free. I've not been completely honest about who I am. Have you heard of Charles Davis?"

"Of course," Jo said, thinking that even someone without a television would know him. He was one of the countries richest men, leading philanthropists, and a local celebrity.

"I'm him," Francis said. "Sort of."

Jo fell silent, her jaw clamped tight. She was confused by his nervous rambling and felt anger starting to rise up.

Francis took another deep breath and attempted to explain. "His words, his speeches, his decisions, the way the billions are allocated, I control all of that."

Jo felt white hot anger swelling inside of her. Secrets. Lies. Francis was the final straw, her one last ditch effort to trust another human being, to live in union with another person. Was he no different than any other man? For a fleeting moment, she wished she hadn't fallen into the habit of leaving her handgun home on Sundays. It would make killing him so much easier, first him and then herself.

Through the fury a single thought came to her, "Breathe." She did. Then another thought, "Be still." She struggled to comply.

Francis glanced her way. For once he was having trouble reading her face, so he plunged ahead. "Would you let me tell the story without interruption, because it is rather long and complicated even if I say it straight through."

She nodded, unable to speak.

"For the past year, I've been telling you about me, about what I do. All the stories I've told, that was me, I was that man driving through Sierra Leone. The Idol initiatives, I funded that. I spend most of my week on airplanes checking on endeavors across the globe and the rest of my time meeting with high level advisors."

"Hang on," he said. "Let me backup. My parents were very, very wealthy people. But they also were extremely private, not attention-grabbing like a Hilton or Leona Hensley, but instead did everything possible to avoid the public eye. They didn't gather much notice because they lived a decent, modest life. My father was a philanthropist and had set up the initial structure of a network to funnel his money into various do-gooding channels without anyone knowing it was coming from him. My mother, not being the bury-talents-in-the-ground type, put the fortune into a combination of bonds and high risk investment. My father's biggest concern during his lifetime and for mine was the protection of privacy."

"Well, anyways…"

Jo examined him wearily, she tried to absorb the information, struggling to make sense of it.

"Oh wait, wait. I forgot to tell you a most important piece. It likely will weigh into your decision. I received access to the trust on my 18th birthday. My aunts had always covered my basic needs, but there was not much more for 'extras' as they called them, like the electronic gadgets or expensive brands of clothing that largely separate the popular from the losers in schoolroom politics. So, when I came into the cash I went nuts. After a three year spree of reckless spending, acquiring an obscene number of big toys, and accumulating an endless list of best friends and a large entourage, I realized, unlike my father, I had no financial constraint. I had become a complete asshole."

"So, in my typical compulsive manner, I had my advisors help me draft a means of making the finances a permanent trust. Basically, I set up rules handing over the trust fund to strictly philanthropic ventures. I wish now I had been a little more generous with my allowance. I had just read "The Perfect Joy of St. Francis" by Felix Timmermans, the life story of my namesake, and was unduly influenced by St. Francis' life of poverty and his earning his own livelihood. This work has been too consuming for me to take on a regular job; I didn't realize this would *be* my income and not just supplement it."

"The money is mine, only I can't spend it on myself, except for things like the suits and the private plane used exclusively in conjunction with business ventures. I receive a small weekly stipend each Friday, usually I've spent that by Wednesday and mooch off my aunts for the remainder of the week. If I marry, the amount will increase to support comfortably, middle-class living, with funds for the children's college."

"Oh, Jo. I'm a servant to this money and I've been asking God for years now to release me from this servitude. To give me a sign. I think he's given it to me. I've picked a successor. No one you would know, conduits like me are invisible by nature. Of course I may have to jump in if he screws up; but he's been working side-by-side with me for two years and frankly I think his judgment is often better than mine."

Finally Jo was able to speak. She took a deep breath and told Francis, "I'm angry right now. If I brought my handgun I might put a bullet through your head."

"Can I give it a plate spin?" Francis implored.

"Go for it."

"The Francis you know, that is who I am. And it's not going to change. This other stuff. Well, that is only what I do. Truthfully it's a hardship. I can't tell you how much I want to give it up."

Francis risked a sidelong look and thought he saw the tension in Jo's face easing ever so slightly.

"There were two reasons I couldn't tell you earlier on. The first is that this is something I could tell only to someone I trusted completely; telling the wrong person would expose me to a life of being hounded by the media and the truly desperate from around the world. This knowledge in the wrong hands would ruin the foundation which depends on my anonymity. So, I had to be sure. The second reason is that I want to walk away from it all. If someone knew and cared about me for my secret billionaire identity, even a little bit, they may resent my decision to bailout and keep me bound to what I've come to see as an encumbrance."

"You don't know how many times I've prayed to God to take away this burden, asking for a sign to know when the time was right and the path to my freedom. I received the sign in a dream that I dreamed again and again. I dreamed of a female warrior with vertical stripes of rust colored war paint on both sides of her face. The dream subsided only when I began to actively seek out this woman. When I found you, it stopped completely."

"I held that image of a woman warrior with a rust streaks beneath her eyes running down each cheek," Francis reiterated. "When I first saw you on the train, I recognized you were the warrior. Later I realized the colored stripes were the grooves you cried as a child and, though your eyes have rusted, the tears you feel inside for the street children you can't reach out to."

"The same day my replacement started working solo, was the very first time I let you see me on the train. I had to wait until I knew he was right before introducing myself. I knew once I got to know you, there would be no going back to my old life."

"Jo," Francis said with a sigh. "It's been a good run, and I've done great things by the grace of God and the mounds of cash at my disposal. But, I'm tired and used up."

Francis then pulled off Route 20 at a brick red sign that read "The Wayside Inn." Seeing the place excited him, and he at least momentarily transitioned from his extraordinary story into his habit of fact sharing about their outing of the week. It was just as well. Jo needed some time to think.

"This is a very special place. It's the country's oldest inn, built in 1716." He kept driving.

"There's the barn," he said as they approached a beautifully restored barn-red barn with a large open door bordered in white, a red fence going across the entrance, and a vent bordered in white above the door.

"And the ice house," he said referring to a grey one-story building near the pond. "They would cut ice from the pond and put it in the house during the winter. It was so well insulated that the ice would last the entire summer and fall."

"Here we are, Josephine Pond," he announced. It was postcard picturesque: there was a line of apple trees with a view of the inn to the left and to the right was a tiny chapel with a white steeple, the kind from a child's drawing or picture book, built from trees felled from the historic hurricane of 1938. In the spring, this was one of the most popular wedding places in New England. On this late Fall day, even though it was an unseasonably warm one, they had the place practically to themselves.

They arrived at a chapel encircled by a meadow of green and brown grasses sprinkled with the season's last harvest of wild flowers. Near the pond, was an enormous, gnarled apple tree. Approaching it they were greeted by the faint smell of fermenting fruit. A few dried apples lay under the tree. The dogs were not accustom to running free and hung at Jo's heels for a while. Then Ben caught scent of a woodcock and, with a little encouragement from Jo, took off at full stride with Rufus galloping after him.

Francis laid out the blanket and put down the picnic basket and the drink cooler. He unpacked cold fried chicken, sandwiches, home-made potato salad, and a tall apple pie. "Wait," Francis remembered, "the china." He laid out china dishes, crystal, and silver silverware. He took a bottle of champagne from the cooler and put it in a silver bucket of half melted ice.

Then Francis held Jo's hands and without taking his eyes off hers, he professed, "I want to live a normal life. I want to settle down with you, support you in collecting waifs through the night, open a school for wayward girls, do some hands on do-gooding, for once, and maybe raise a half dozen kids of our own. Of course there's more," he went on. "But that's basically it."

They were both sitting. Francis without loosening his hold, shifted onto one knee. For once they were at the same height, seeing eye-to-eye.

"So…Will you marry me?" Francis asked Jo.

Jo had no idea whether all of this was so or whether he was an amazingly creative albeit deluded storyteller. Suddenly it struck her. What did it matter? Either way, she felt an inability to walk away from him any more than from a stray with a busted leg looking at her through soulful eyes.

"Yes," Jo answered with conviction.

He took Jo in his arms and held her close. It felt so good. Over the past year, Jo had been becoming increasingly aware of emptiness in her life, a void, and one that Francis filled perfectly. She hugged him tightly, for once not holding back. She forgot for a moment how strong she was. Affection turned into pain, but Francis didn't seem to care. Now that her mind was made, Jo's desire for Francis was greater than ever. She already knew she didn't want him to go home tonight.

Releasing him she gestured toward the chapel grudgingly, "I don't suppose we could round up a minister."

"Well," said Francis. "We have an appointment for 2:00."

"I made one, just in case," he confessed.

Jo and Francis sat in the November sun partly shaded by the tree branches stretching out above them. Jo had questions but decided not to bombard Francis with them. There would be time for that later. A warm and sunny autumn day in New England, perhaps the last until next spring, was not to be wasted. They clinked crystal goblets and sipped deeply from their sparkling drinks, sitting in the early afternoon breeze, listening to the songs of birds.

Francis looked at his watch and said. "It's time."

Jo responded. "Let's do this."

Francis packed up their lunch remnants, and Jo folded the blanket. Standing first, Francis reached out his hand to help Jo up and then held on, walking hand-in-hand to the church. It was a classical old New England chapel with a tall steeple and a semi-circular red brick walkway leading to the entrance. To the right was the water wheel of the grist mill, slowly churning by the current of the small stream that wound through the grounds.

Jo hadn't heard other cars arrive, but four more had joined Francis' Nova in the lot. When they walked inside, Jo saw sitting in the pews a small team of people with portable equipment to sample blood and notarize forms.

"I told you I know people," said Francis.

Jo thought suddenly of Jay Yarmo and Simon Cowell, and wondered just how many people, and who, Francis knew. A nurse was there who expertly extracted small vials of blood. The town clerk from Sudbury pointed out where to sign a number of forms and collected them.

"I don't come out on a Sunday for everyone, Francis," she said. "But after all you've done for the town, for this place, well, it's the least I could do. There's a three day cooling off period. Then you can be married in any town or city in the Commonwealth within the next thirty days."

When the legalities were completed everyone but the witness, who was seated toward the back, left, wishing Francis the best of luck and congratulating and smiling at Jo. Together, hand-in-hand, Jo and Francis approached the altar. The entire back wall of the chapel was glass looking out onto the meadow surrounded by woods. In the distance Jo could see the apple tree where she and Francis had just picnicked. The window and outdoors beyond framed a short Episcopal priest with silvery white hair. It was difficult to assess her exact size or shape within in a linen colored robe. The sash over her neck showed images of animals and plants in shades of green puzzled together into a pattern, it looked like it was hand stitched.

"Hello Jo. My name is Vicar Pat Huess, I baptized Francis. So," she said with a smile, "I've known him for a little while. I'm assuming since you are here that you're engaged."

They both nodded.

"Okay. Let's get started. Francis, Jo, you just stand here." Ben and Rufus not to miss out on the festivities made a dash to the altar, and Rufus almost knocked the priest over. "No worries. I have two dogs of my own. You should've seen our church a last month, for the feast of St. Francis–we have the blessing of the pets and our little church was teaming with animals. Your boys are part of your family and should share in this wonderful day."

Rufus took a few laps up and down the aisles before throwing himself on the foot of the altar, panting heavily. Ben sat straight and still next to Francis, who thought he couldn't have asked for a more suitable best man. Jo and Francis released their hands and then turned slightly to face one another and with the priest made a triangle.

Jo surveyed the chapel. It was basic, but elegant, with 12 boxed rows on each side. Above the alter was a simple, wooden cross, similar to the one Francis wore, but wall-sized. She felt comfortable here.

"A betrothment ceremony is one of the church's oldest traditions," the priest began. "In the early church when there were arranged marriages, it was often the first time a bride and groom met each other. In the 19th century it was a required part of the process of marriage. Today, couples use this ceremony as a sign that they understand the sanctity of marriage and the enormity of their commitment. Jo and Francis, you come before the Lord to affirm your engagement and your devotion to each other. Our first reading is from the Gospel of Luke Chapter twelve."

Jo was half listening to the reading. She had a lot on her mind. The part that stuck was God's knowing the number of hairs on her head. Jo wondered if the count changed whenever a strand fell out or grew in and marveled that anyone would care to know her so intimately. Afterwards, the priest talked of the worth of a sparrow which made Jo think of each pigeon that had been nursed to health or died with dignity in Jo's bedroom rescue.

The priest continued. "The next reading is from Mathew, Chapter thirteen." Jo listened politely to the parable of the mustard seed, but was drawn in by the end of the reading. During this part Francis' eyes gleamed as he fixed his gaze on Jo as though for the first time. "The kingdom of heaven is like a merchant looking for great pearls. When he found one of great value, he went away and sold everything he had and bought it." That's what Francis did, she reasoned. He gave away everything he had, she still was fuzzy as to what or whether he'd gotten a pearl out of the deal. Francis still couldn't take his eyes off her. Every time the word "pearl" was said, his head bobbed in her direction. Maybe she was it? Or at least part of it. Maybe the pearl was their lives together? Or perhaps it was participating together in some greater good, a plan or a lot of plans orchestrated by God himself. Yes, that was it. Somehow, she felt sure of it.

After the reading, Quique, the man who was seated in the tenth row, arose from his seat. He approached them with a guitar in hand. He was about Francis' age. Jo had thought, when she first saw him from a distance, that he was Italian. Up-close she could see he was Spanish. Or of mixed descent. He looked as though he were walking straight out of the pages of a fashion magazine. He was impeccably groomed so as to achieve a rugged male look, including each windswept hair in place and a purposeful 72 hour stubble. He had deep brown eyes with gold-flecked rings and a quiet demeanor.

As Quique strapped on his guitar, Jo realized that, obviously, he was an entertainer, not a witness. Jo braced herself for a sentimental ballad. Francis could be such a sap at times. She supposed, though, that this was not the time for sarcasm. Swallowing the biting remark forming on her tongue, she closed her eyes to better hear the words. She tried to keep an open mind.

Francis enjoyed a rare opportunity to stare intently and freely at Jo. She looked exactly as he always imagined her: serene. He drank in her beauty and explored each nuance of her exquisite face. In that moment, as he awaited in excited anticipation her reaction to the song, he was filled with joy to overflowing.

Quique started with a familiar pop song tune as he whispered the words in Jo's direction: "Would you dance?..."

Jo thought his voice sounded just like a performer on the radio.

"Hmm…" she tried to remember. "What was his

name?"

Quique had amazing talent; his acoustic rendition sounded even better than the radio. He had a rich, smooth tone. He sang some of the words in a tremor and held onto others just long enough to express a passionate, limitless, and never-ending desire for another, the one other.

From the first sung line, Jo realized these were not lyrics she'd heard before. And, clearly they were words written for her. These were Francis' wedding vows.

"Would you twirl, if you saw I was there?
Could I lope with you through the night?
Would you weep, if you knew how I care?
Kiss me in your arms tonight.

"I will stand beside you always.
I will share in all your pain.
I will hold you through the bad times.
I give you all that I am."

As the verses continued and the chorus replayed, Jo let the music wash over her and the words reach her. She still was not completely accustomed to Francis' exposing his heart. His honesty and outspoken feelings for her were at times overwhelming. But on this day, she soaked in his words like a renewing rain.

As the song came to a close, Francis gave Jo's hands a tight squeeze.

Releasing them, he turned to the singer and said, "Hey, Quique, I appreciate your coming up. I know you have to run."

"No problem, man," he replied, removing the strap and still holding onto the neck of his guitar.

He exchanged a three quarters side-on embrace with Francis, and they clapped each other roughly on the shoulders.

Jo overheard Francis say, "And just talk to Philip about whatever you need for Haiti."

Taking a step back Quique nodded to Jo, and with a quick "Ciao Bella," he slipped out the back exit.

Sometime later, Jo would hear the whole story of how songwriter Enrique Iglesias co-wrote with Francis the lyrics to their vows and sang at her wedding. For now, even without that knowledge, Jo thought the lingering melody of their wedding hopes and promises was the most wonderful and welcome gift imaginable.

It was just the three of them. Francis immediately returned his full attention to Jo. The priest continued the ceremony with a scripture she knew was a favorite of Francis.' At the same time she wanted to respect Jo's discomfort with the word "love."

Vicar Huess said. "Next, we have a selection adapted from 1 Corinthians Chapter thirteen." Since God is love, the scripture read like this:

God is patient and kind;
God does not envy or boast;
God is not arrogant or rude.
God does not insist on His own way;
God is not irritable or resentful;
God does not rejoice at wrongdoing, but rejoices with the truth.
God bears all things, believes all things, hopes all

things, endures all things."

Francis took from his pocket two dollar store rings. He had explained to the priest beforehand that these were "fillers" and he planned to buy, somehow, whatever ring Jo picked out. The priest told Francis the blessing would carry though from these symbolic pieces to the real thing, no worries.

"Bless these rings, O Lord, as a sign of the vows that this man and this woman take when they bind themselves to each other through Jesus Christ our Lord."

A little religious, Jo thought, but it was church after all, and Francis was happy. The priest ended with "Francis and Jo, you are now betrothed in the eyes of the church and the Lord."

The couple hugged, then kissed deeply. Francis, after taking a moment to recover and before growing too excited, made a quick check on whether there were lingering rules, "What about the cooling off period?"

Jo returned. "As far as you, me, and God are concerned, we've made our choice. As for the state of Massachusetts well, I really don't give a...," she paused, "damn?" Francis nodded, thinking while it might, perhaps, be a sinful thing for him to say, for Jo it was a definite improvement. They kissed again. And again.

They thanked the priest who embraced them both. Vicar Pat reminded them to meet her Wednesday at 10:00 at Boston City Hall to exchange legal vows and pick up the license. Jo and Francis loaded the picnic supplies and two tired dogs into the car and headed back into the city. Francis and Jo still wore the dollar-a-piece rings Francis brought for the ceremony. He guessed right that Jo would want to pick out their wedding rings. She said she wanted to do it right away.

Jo told him. "I know a place."

Jo and Francis stopped briefly at the aunts' tiny house, where Francis picked up three cleaned and pressed suits, a pair of shined shoes, a change of casual clothes, a pair of pajamas, his laptop, a briefcase, and toiletries packed in a leather travel case. After disentangling themselves from the embrace of the aunts, who cycled between screaming, crying, and laughing, they headed for Jo's apartment. There they dropped off the dogs and Francis' belongings. Then, Jo and Francis took two subway trains to a not so nice part of the city.

On the way, Jo sent a single text announcement. "Hey Nick guess what? Just married Francis–let's all get together to celebrate."

Jo led the way down a side street. The sun was setting and questionable people were emerging onto the street.

"I'll keep an eye out for you," Jo reassured him. "Some of these ladies are eying you like a stray dog for a cheeseburger."

Francis figured it was not a Barmakian jewelers she had in mind. He suspected they'd be selecting rings from a pawn shop. Jo stopped in front of a store

Spin the Plate

front with iron bars over the windows and a neon sign that read "Sins on Skins."

She explained. "Our shop isn't open on Sunday, but I figured one of these sketchier places would be."

"Most tattoo places, though are basically the same," Jo said. "Tons of designs all over the walls and a front part that looks like a waiting room at a doctor's office."

Francis thought this one was more like a free clinic.

Looking around, Jo said under her breath. "The clients are pretty much the same too: tough dudes coming out with tears in their eyes and people getting one stage completed of huge tattoos that go all down their backs. And, there are always some chicks getting cute flowers or hearts."

As they sat in the waiting room Francis asked Jo to talk him through it.

"It won't take that long," she explained. "Not more than 5 to 10 minutes for small ones like these, and a one time thing."

"What does it feel like?" Francis asked.

"It hurts," she said.

Jo's name was called and the two disappeared into the back. The artist was the stereotypical burly, hairy, tattoo covered, leather clad man. Seated at his left was a muscular Rottweiler.

Jo called out a greeting. "Hi there Spike."

Francis wasn't sure if she was addressing the man or the dog. Despite the several half empty drink bottles and discarded food wrappers littering the room, Francis somehow felt he could trust this person to stick needles into him. The man said he'd have to shave the skin first since there is hair all over the body, even on the back of the finger.

First though was the design. They talked to "Spike" about getting the rings, and he showed them some options. Francis was relieved to hear that tattoo rings are not done all the way around the finger, just on the back. The skin on the inside of the finger sheds constantly so any tattoo there would fade fast. That was fine by him: less tattoo, less pain.

Jo and Francis looked at a number of designs and didn't like any of them enough. Francis was partial to a wave design, but it was something they wanted to agree on. So, Jo ended up designing the pattern for them. She traced her and Francis' hand on a piece of paper so that he too could visualize what was in her head. She relayed to him her image of two hands reaching and fingertips touching, merging under a mighty protection as she sketched two black lines with three dots above them. Using a black felt tip pen, she drew the same design for both, making hers more feminine with thinner lines and the dots smaller; on her ring there were tinier dots on each side. The result was simple, but somehow profound.

Francis knew it would hurt, but figured that this was as good a way as any to embark upon on a lifelong commitment. Jo went first and showed no reaction, nor emotion. Then, it was Francis' turn.

Jo's description of the experience was spot on, "It feels like being burned while a bee stings you over and over again."

Francis knew if he moved and the design got

messed up he'd have that mess for the rest of his life. So, he stayed still fighting the pain.

"Don't be a wus," he told himself, holding back tears that he could feel at the back of his eyeballs.

When it was done, the fresh tattoo looked crisp and sharp. Jo told him that it wouldn't always look that way.

"When the scab falls off," Jo said. "It will look a little dull, but by then," she assured him, "you'll love it so much you won't care."

Francis hoped Jo would always feel the same way about him.

CHAPTER 10: The Dream

That night Jo lay asleep in her bed... *and suddenly there he was, coming towards her, carrying a dollhouse stretched out across two arms, enormous, pinkness, him peering over the side, an excited grin.*

Jo was jolted awake as though from a free-falling dream, the instant before hitting the pavement. She backed her large frame into the curve of Francis' sinewy one. Francis draped his arm across her and sleepily kissed the nape of her neck. She twisted to face him, and he drew her into his arms. His rhythmic breath warmed her shoulder as he slept.

Jo repeated to herself. "Oh God keep me safe, make me strong," as she drew in a long breath and exhaled deeply.

Jo was unafraid. She thought back to the dollhouse episode. She allowed it to play through to the end. Rather than the terror or rage she normally experienced, she felt pity for a father who had squandered all he was given. In a moment of clarity, Jo saw the enormity of the blessings in her life. She was determined not to make the same mistakes her parents had. She randomly picked another episode: number 68. Again, there was a bit of sadness, but no pain. Then 125, 87, 4. Nothing. It was as though she were watching the scene, but for once was not a part of it. She cut-off episode 4 half-way through. The psychological chains that held her prisoner for so long had dissolved.

She resisted the urge to nudge Francis awake. Tomorrow she would tell him the wondrous news. "Francis, when I think of the episodes, I don't feel anything." Speechless, for once, he would hold her tight and cry joyful tears as he moved this answered prayer onto the praise and thanksgiving list he kept in his mind. Jo was free.

She felt her pounding heart slow with a sudden and absolute knowledge. "It is finished."

Then, she received an idea. "Stay here in the now."

To pull herself into the present Jo reached for a mental joy fix. She turned her mind to a vision of the foolish rattie boys running free. She breathed in deeply and exhaled slowly. The rats were playing in a field of grasses and wildflowers, a ways off in the distance. Then, catching sight of her, they scampered towards her for tickles and some peanut butter toast.

It was then Jo heard. "And see the to be," as the rats stood up on two legs, and with outstretched arms grew into humans, girls, rushing her, hugging. She knew in that moment that she would have a second childhood; one lived through the eyes of her own children. She would experience nurturing mothering; she would be that mother for them.

She gathered the girls up in her arms murmuring into course hair. "I will keep you safe, make you strong."

Jo drifted into a peaceful sleep.

EPILOGUE

Jo sat at her dressing table with her back to the mirror facing a teenage girl who was brushing peach blush lightly along the side of Jo's face. Erin was not Jo and Francis' youngest child, though she was the most immature of their girls and the newest addition to the family. Behind Erin, on Jo's dresser was a framed photograph of all five sisters.

Francis poked his head into the bedroom. He was dressed in his Louis of Boston tuxedo and carrying a slice of cheese pizza.

"Pizza's here," he announced taking a bite.

"Francis, that's for the girls. You know this is a dinner thing," Jo reminded him.

"I was hungry! It's just a snack," he said with his mouth full, hurrying back to the kitchen to do some crowd control.

Jo thought Francis looked fine in his new tux and with the extra 25 pounds he put on since he discovered snacking. Erin did not join the other girls scrambling for the largest, cheesiest slices in the kitchen. She continued sketching the edges of Jo's mouth with lip liner.

Jo gazed at the picture of the girls on her dresser. Had it really been a year? It was hard to remember a life without Francis; it seemed that they had been together forever. And yet, she remembered every detail of the day he proposed, as though it happened yesterday. Jo examined the photo of their five adopted children. She noted that the girls were seated not by height or age but by seniority: first Naran now16 with silky black hair, dark almond eyes, and the same slight build as when Jo had first encountered her during the street fight so many nights ago; Tanya, their oldest, with rich coffee, no cream colored skin, tight braids, and a biting sense of humor; Shaina who by her dental exam was 11 or 12; Sarai, also 12, orphaned in Sierra Leone who danced as she walked and was effortlessly picking up the English language and US social customs; and finally 14 year old Erin.

Erin stepped back and took a critical look at her work. One half of Jo's face was more peachy than the other. She added another coat of blush to the left side.

"This will bring out your high cheek bones," Erin said knowingly, quoting Carmindy, the stylist on the makeover show she watched with Jo every Friday night. "And done."

Jo twisted around to gaze at her reflection.

"Wow, I look hot," Jo remarked.

Erin glowed under the praise. But as Jo stood, the girl suddenly became nervous. Erin had been pacified up to this point by being allowed to do Jo's hair and make-up, but with the distraction complete her resolve waned.

"Can't you stay home tonight until I fall asleep, like always," Erin whined.

Jo could relate to the girl's need for regular

routine, but said, "No, not tonight. You know Daddy and I need to go listen to his speech. Your aunties are already here and will take good care of you."

"Will Angie be coming home tonight?" Erin asked.

"I hope so my little lovey," Jo responded, pushing the girl's overgrown bangs off her forehead. "It's her choice, but if I can find her tonight I'll invite her again."

"Tell her I miss her," Erin asked.

"I always do," Jo assured her.

Jo settled back into her chair. She gazed up at the adolescent standing in front of her, and the corners of her mouth upturned slightly. She stretched out her arms, and Erin immediately launched herself into them. Wrapping her arms around the girl, Jo breathed in the sweet scent of cherry blossom body spray and Herbal Essence shampoo as mother and daughter shared a long, unhurried embrace.

Spin the Plate

© Black Rose Writing

Breinigsville, PA USA
13 June 2010
239716BV00001B/1/P